ASH

SILVER SAINTS MC

FIONA DAVENPORT

Copyright © 2025 by Fiona Davenport

Cover designed by Elle Christensen

Edited by Jenny Sims (Editing4Indies)

All rights reserved.

No part of this book may be reproduced in any form or by any electronic or mechanical means, including information storage and retrieval systems, without written permission from the author, except for the use of brief quotations in a book review.

 Created with Vellum

ASH
HOUNDS OF HELLFIRE MC

As the lawyer for the Hounds of Hellfire MC, Elias "Ash" Prescott III was usually a smooth talker. But his way with words failed him when it came to the sassy EMT who took care of his bullet wound.

Nora Stoll was not impressed when Ash asked her out the first time. Or when he stood her up after he finally talked her into a date. But when she's taken by criminals in need of medical care, she knew Ash would come for her.

PROLOGUE

ASH

"Son of a bitch!" I roared as I staggered backward, my shoulder on fucking fire. The bitch had shot me!

My club brothers, Wizard and Echo, disarmed her while I checked the wound. It wasn't deep and probably only needed a few stitches, but the bullet was still lodged inside. The wound hurt like a motherfucker.

"Ash?" Echo called.

I tore off a strip of fabric from my shirt and pressed it over the hole in my arm to control the bleeding.

"The safety was off?" Cynthia shrieked at the top of her lungs, drowning out my response. Her voice was shaking with panic. "Oh, fuck. Did I kill him? Shit!"

Figured she'd freak the fuck out. Her real name was Jean, and she was the con artist, burglar, and gold digger we'd set up. She was a shrew but not a killer. I took sinister pleasure in the fact that she was listening to the sirens getting closer and terrified that she was gonna go down for murder.

I looked over at where Wizard and Echo had her restrained. Thankfully, despite being a tech genius, Wizard was tough as shit. Echo, a surveillance specialist, was also our Road Captain and as lethal as the rest of us.

She struggled like a lunatic—which didn't seem that far off at this point—and screamed, "Let me go! I'll kill you! Let me go, you bastards!"

"Ash!" Echo shouted again, demanding a response.

"Yeah, yeah. Just a fucking nick," I grunted. It was bleeding pretty profusely, so the wound looked worse than it was. I dropped onto a chair in the living room that was open to the hallway, so I still had eyes on the action in case the guys needed an extra hand.

A relieved breath whooshed from Echo's lungs, but then Cynthia's elbow landed hard on his sternum.

I winced. *Fucking ouch.*

"Wiz..." he gasped, his eyes glazing over from a lack of oxygen. "Take...can't...oh, fuck." He tried to choke in some air unsuccessfully, then hit the floor.

Thankfully, Wizard had her in a fierce grip.

I couldn't help barking out a laugh when Echo hit the floor. He was gonna get so much shit for that.

Cynthia was whining and spitting curses, making my head hurt. I was so fucking tired of being around her.

She was the head of a con ring who'd been taking people's life savings. Unfortunately for her, one of her underlings had set his eye on Echo's woman.

Messing with my MC, the Hounds of Hellfire, was stupid as fuck, but going after an old lady was signing your death warrant. She was lucky we'd decided to only ruin her and get her arrested. But we didn't want her disappearance bringing heat down on us since her organization was pretty big.

King, our president, had talked me into playing the part of her next mark.

I was the club secretary and lawyer, but I'd been born into a very wealthy family. My father was a Texas politician, and my mother was more concerned with her status in society than her only child. With a platform heavily focused on family values, having a kid had been good for their image. Otherwise, I probably wouldn't exist.

They'd expected me to follow in their footsteps, which meant they were ecstatic when I decided I wanted to attend law school.

But I wasn't interested in being their fucking puppet. So I'd worked my ass off to be a straight A student and got scholarships to cover my bachelor's and law degree. I worked for anything I needed and didn't take a single cent from them.

Obviously, they weren't happy when I decided to work as a public defender, but they managed to "spin" it to make themselves look good.

That got shot to hell when I patched with the Hounds. I gained a real family, one where bonds were forged by something stronger than blood. It was just a perk that my parents cut me out of their life.

But my background was the perfect cover to get Cynthia's attention.

We played up my role as the senator's son—making it look like I'd simply been a recluse all the years since I dropped out of the media.

My brothers thought it was hysterical when my parents called, trying to reconnect. They'd thought I'd changed my tune and was returning to their society. Obviously, they wanted to take advantage of the situation or clean it up, depending on my motives. I told them to go fuck themselves and hung up.

I'd taken Cynthia to a black-tie charity event and let her record my voice, thinking she was creating a key to my safe without my knowledge. Then Echo had concocted a bullshit excuse about my dad being in the hospital to give me a reason to bolt.

I hadn't been amused.

We staked out "my house" and waited for her to break into my server room and hack my bank accounts. While she transferred the funds—which were tagged so we could follow the money to all of her accounts and assets—we called the police.

Getting her for attempted murder was an unexpected plus.

The police burst in the door, and I scowled when EMTs followed them. *Fuck.* They were gonna be a pain in the ass.

"Sir. Hello, my name is Nora. I'm here to help. Are you alright?" My head whipped around at the sweet, musical voice.

Bright blue eyes stared at me with concern as she approached me. Her pale skin was sprinkled with adorable freckles, emphasized by the long red hair twisted into a bun thing on the back of her head.

The gorgeous EMT was tall, but at six three, I

still had at least half a foot on her. Her body was athletic, but she still managed to look sweet and fragile. Her mouthwatering tits were high and round, not big, but perfect for my hands and mouth. Damn, her body would fit against mine like they'd been made from the same mold.

But as I studied her a little more, I realized she was young. Too fucking young. I probably had fifteen years on her, at least.

She was also too innocent for the world I lived in. Not to mention all the filthy ways I wanted to fuck her.

Nora knelt in front of me, and I gulped as I tried to hide my reaction from the onslaught of dirty thoughts that hit me. Her Cupid's bow mouth would look amazing wrapped around my cock.

"Holy cow!" she exclaimed. "You've been shot!"

A lazy smile curved up my lips. "I've had worse."

Her concerned expression turned into confusion until she clocked my crooked grin, then she rolled her eyes and turned away to unzip her bag. "I don't want to know," she muttered as she withdrew a pair of sterile gloves and put them on. "Right now, I'm only concerned with your current wound."

"Nothing to worry over, baby girl," I murmured. "Just a nick. My friend over there needs you more than I do." The statement left a dirty taste in my mouth and made me feel a little homicidal. *What the fuck was that?*

"Why don't you let the person with medical training assess your wound before making assumptions?" she snapped, turning back to me with gauze in hand.

I pulled away the cloth I'd been using to stanch the bleeding and replaced it with the gauze. When she put pressure on the wound, I winced, and her eyes narrowed on me.

"Turn around so I can locate the exit wound," she instructed, her tone stiff, making me silently chuckle. I was pretty sure she felt the same spark between us and was fighting it. I wanted to push her to admit it, but there was no point when we had such a huge chasm, and I didn't only mean our age difference.

When Nora gently took hold of my arm, I remembered she wouldn't find anything on the back. And I was pretty sure that if she knew the bullet was still inside, she'd use any and all tactics to get me to the hospital.

Hospitals reported gunshot wounds. The club had two patches who were qualified doctors, and they were used to this kind of shit; gunshots, stabbing, broken bones from physical fights or weapons, motorcycle accidents...and other stuff that would make a hospital suspicious. And eventually, the police weren't gonna believe the innocent lies we'd have to concoct. Even though they were already involved in this takedown, it was better if I didn't draw too much attention to myself.

"Told you, baby girl, just a nick. No need to make a fuss over me. At least, not about this."

She glanced up at me, and her blue eyes clouded with suspicion. "What is that supposed to mean?"

I winked. "Let me take you to dinner, and we'll talk about it." *Why the hell did you just ask her out, idiot?*

Her lips pinched, and she glared at me with annoyance written all over her face. "Dinner at the hospital cafeteria? No thanks."

My lips curled down. "Who said anything about the cafeteria?"

Nora's eyes blinked innocently, and her tone was overly sweet when she replied, "Where else? You're going to be in the hospital."

I almost laughed at her response. She was definitely innocent and sweet, but there was a little spitfire in there too. I was pretty sure my little vixen was a virgin, and fucking hell...I wanted to be the one who popped her cherry and freed that fire in bed.

"Not going to the hospital, baby girl," I informed her, my tone final.

"I really think—"

"Forget it."

"But—"

"Baby girl," I warned, "if you don't drop this subject, I have many creative ways to shut you up." A wicked smile curved my mouth. "Although, I promise you'll enjoy every one of them."

She gasped. "That's—that's—how dare you. You—you—you presumptuous dingus!"

My eyebrows hit my hairline, and a laugh burst from my chest. "You're adorable, baby girl," I told her, surprised when she frowned.

Then her back straightened, and she stood before looking down her nose at me. "For your information, Mr....Mr...."

"Ash," I inserted for her.

"Mr....Ash. No woman wants to be described as 'adorable,'" she said with a haughty sniff.

"Okay. How about cute?"

"No. Not that either."

"I see. Going more for something like gorgeous?

Sexy? Fuckable? Because you're all of those, baby girl."

A deep blush stained her cheeks, and she tried to look stern, but her blue eyes sparked with pleasure.

"Perhaps. But not by a stranger who is too dumb to accept that he should go to the freaking hospital."

Echo moaned, clearly coming around, and Nora glanced in his direction.

Her partner was already beside him, but she called his name, and he looked up.

"Can you check this guy's vitals? He seems fine, but I'd like a second opinion. I'll handle the other one."

He glanced at Echo, then back at her with confusion, then shrugged. "Sure."

She faced me and gave me a brittle smile. "I hope you don't die, Mr....um, Ash. Have a nice day." She pivoted just as her partner arrived.

He tried to keep his voice down, but I heard him tease, "Pawning the difficult one off to me, Stoll?"

She paused and leaned in to whisper, "He asked me out."

"Another one?" her partner asked, his face screwing up in annoyance.

Another one? How many guys have asked her out

on the job? I was gonna find them all and beat the shit out of them.

Nora nodded, and I completely ignored her partner, watching her kneel beside Echo as he blinked. She pulled a flashlight from her pocket and shined it in his eyes.

"Shit! Stop shining that thing before I go blind," he muttered as he sucked in lungfuls of air.

"You fainted, man," I told him before bursting into laughter.

Nora sighed and shot me a disgruntled frown. "He didn't faint, you butthead. His brain shut off from a lack of oxygen. There's a difference."

"Not when I tell the story," I choked out through my chortling.

"Sir?" Nora said more quietly. "Can you sit up and open your eyes? I just want to make sure you don't have a concussion from the fall."

She checked his pupils, then gave him a soft smile.

I hated it. I wanted all her smiles to be for me.

"Doesn't look like a concussion," she decided. "That was a hard hit you took to the chest. How's your breathing?"

He nodded. "I'm sore, but nothing seems to be obstructing my flow of oxygen."

"Good," she replied with a smile. "I'd prefer to take you to the hospital to be checked out and just make sure she didn't crack your sternum. But..." She scowled at me. "With how freaking stubborn your friend is after being *shot*, I'm guessing a little pain in the chest is nothing compared to dealing with that... pain in the butt."

He chuckled and nodded, earning himself a high spot on my shit list—he'd made it on the list for making her laugh. "You're right on all accounts..." He looked at her expectantly.

I didn't want him to know her name, but that was illogical.

"Oh, my name is Nora," she told him with another smile, making my chest burn with jealousy.

"Well, Nora. You're doubly right. Ash is a pain in the ass, and it's unlikely you'll talk me into going to the hospital."

She sighed and shook her head.

"I promise to get checked out, though, okay?" he offered.

She crooked up one corner of her mouth and gave him a small wave. "I'm going to give you the benefit of the doubt and believe you. It will help me sleep better at night."

He laughed and turned away, only to see me glaring at him.

"What?" he asked, his head tilting to the side as he observed me curiously.

"Nothing," I gritted out. My jaw was so tight, I wouldn't have been surprised if I broke a few teeth.

My attention was stolen by Nora as she walked past me. My hand shot out, but my grip was gentle when I pulled her to a stop. "Only one you should be dreaming about tonight is me, baby girl."

She stiffened and raised her chin to a stubborn angle. "Dream on," she snapped.

"Oh, I will," I murmured before releasing her.

I watched her walk away, my mind swirling with conflicting feelings and trying to figure out where to go from here.

But all it took was seeing her disappear out the door to make up my mind.

Nothing was gonna stop me from making Nora mine.

1

NORA

"On our way," my partner replied to the dispatcher as I changed lanes to make a quick left turn.

I was normally up for just about any call from dispatch for our ambulance, but the moment I heard the address of the one we just got, I cringed.

"Can't we fob the call off to another rig?" I asked, blinking my eyes innocently at him.

Mark shook his head with a sigh. "You're gonna run into the guy at some point. Wouldn't you rather it was when you knew it was gonna happen? That's better than being surprised."

I wasn't happy with his reply, but I knew he was right. "I suppose."

"Are you ever gonna forgive him for standing you up?"

The topic of our conversation was Elias Prescott III, known as Ash to most people—the road name he'd been given by his motorcycle club. Although we didn't know each other well, the first time he called me, I was one of the few he'd given permission to call him Eli instead. But only after he'd apologized for asking me out while I was at work. It'd been effective, too, helping to sway me into believing he was sincere when he apologized because I knew it was a big deal in his world. I had no clue how he got my number. He just said he had his ways.

Shrugging, I murmured, "I don't know. It's not easy when I already had to forgive him for being a butthead when we met."

Mark chuckled. "You gotta give him a little credit for that one. He'd just been shot, and he apologized for asking you out at an inappropriate time."

"I know, which was why I took your advice and forgave him for that." I cast an accusing glance at him. "And look where that got me."

"It's not as though the guy didn't call you to let you know he wasn't gonna make your date," Mark pointed out.

We had already discussed this yesterday, but I

hadn't been willing to listen to reason because the hurt had been too fresh. Now, I didn't have much choice since I would see Eli soon. "Not until thirty minutes before, though. As far as I'm concerned, it was the same thing as standing me up and doesn't exactly inspire confidence in his ability to commit to a relationship."

Mark quirked a brow. "If you're already thinking in terms of a serious relationship, then you and I both know that you're going to need to find a way to get past this and put the guy out of his misery."

I jutted my chin out. "Doesn't mean I can't give him heck so he learns not to take me for granted."

"I'm not gonna argue with you on that." He shook his head with a chuckle. "Susan did the same thing with me when we were first dating, and it's something we've taught the girls, too."

"Start how you plan to go on." His daughters weren't the only ones he'd given this advice to. I flashed him a quick grin as I made the turn onto the road where the Hounds of Hellfire compound was located.

"That's right, but I don't think you need to be worried about Ash not being willing to put in the work to build something with you. Look how much effort he's put in over the past two weeks."

"Fine," I huffed, thinking about all of the texts Eli had sent since he bailed on our date. "If he's there and wants to talk, I guess I can give him the chance to at least apologize in person. Again."

Mark beamed an approving smile at me. "Atta girl."

I'd been incredibly lucky when our ambulance company paired me with Mark. He'd been my mentor during my hands-on training and volunteered to be my partner when I'd been hired after passing the national certification exam. I couldn't have asked to be paired with a better paramedic. Something I reminded myself of when I pulled through the gates and parked the ambulance in front of the clubhouse. Eli might have all his Hounds of Hellfire members to support him when we went in there, but at least I had Mark.

Knowing I was reluctant to speak with Eli, my partner headed straight for the guys after we made it inside. He asked them what was going on while I headed straight for the woman on a barstool with a big guy hovering over her. With the details the dispatcher had given us, it was safe to assume she was our patient. "You don't look so good. Is there any medical history I need to know about or pre-existing conditions?"

"Nope, I've always been as healthy as a horse."

"That's good to hear." Hoping to ease the concern that was clear in her eyes, I flashed her a quick smile before pulling a blood pressure cuff out of my trauma bag. "I'm Nora. What's your name?"

"Thea."

"Enough chitchat," the big guy barked. "What's wrong with my woman?

"Careful."

If the warning had come from anyone other than Eli, I would've at least flashed them an appreciative smile, but I refused to let him distract me from my job. So I focused on taking Thea's vitals. "Is there any chance you're pregnant?"

"A whole lot of them," she confirmed. "But only over the past two weeks, so isn't it too soon for me to be having symptoms like this?"

"Nope." My lips curved as I repacked my equipment into my bag, happy that the most likely outcome was something wonderful. "Your blood pressure is normal. Same with your temperature and pulse ox."

Thea looked relieved as she murmured, "That's good to hear."

"The dizziness passed fairly quickly, and it's often one of the first symptoms a woman experiences during pregnancy since it can be caused by hormonal changes or increased blood volume," I explained, using all of my self-control to keep my gaze on her face without glancing up at Eli. But I didn't manage to resist the impulse to poke at him verbally. "My recommendation is that you have your man send his friend out for a pregnancy test and take it as soon as possible."

Her brows drew together as she asked, "His friend?"

"That one." I pointed at Eli without needing to look at him since I was much too aware of the man. "It'll probably embarrass him, which would be awesome."

"Wouldn't be bothered by it at all, Nora," Eli disagreed.

I somehow managed to keep my focus on Thea as I advised, "If the test is positive, make an appointment with your gynecologist. If it's negative, go in to see your primary care physician, even if you don't get faint again. Better be safe than sorry."

Her man squeezed her shoulder. "She'll see a doctor soon, either way."

"Good."

With that reassurance, I headed back out to the ambulance with Eli following me. After I tossed my trauma bag in the back, Mark held his hand out. "Gimme the keys. I'll fill out the PCR while you give the man a chance to apologize face-to-face for fucking up again."

The smile Eli had aimed Mark's way at the start of my partner's statement quickly turned into a glare at the end. Laughing, I handed over the keys to the rig before turning toward the man I hadn't been able to stop thinking about over the past two weeks, even when I was mad at him.

Considering Eli was six feet and three inches of pure muscle—combined with buzzed black hair, a short-cropped beard, tan skin, hazel eyes, and a killer smile—I didn't think any woman alive would judge me for being mildly obsessed with the guy. Not even with how much he'd managed to mess up with me in such a short time.

"Missed seeing your gorgeous face these past two weeks," Eli murmured as he prowled closer.

With the ambulance doors at my back, there was nowhere for me to go, so I stood my ground. "You could've seen it a few nights ago if you'd shown up for our date, you blundering dunderhead."

Ignoring my insult—which irritated me since I found it quite creative—he clenched his fists at his side. "You have no idea how much I fucking hated having to make that call. If there had been any way to get out of the club business I had to attend to, I would have done it. But it wasn't something I could hand off to anyone else since I'm the club's legal counsel."

"You mentioned that when you called less than thirty minutes before our date," I muttered, hitching my hip against the rear bumper of the ambulance.

"Which just about killed me, Nora." He pressed a hand against his chest. "I hated knowing I'd hurt you. Even more than I've despised not being able to talk to you since then."

"It really sucks that you're so good with your words." Which was why I'd avoided talking to him until I had a chance to really think about if I wanted to give him another chance without the undue influence he wielded over me. Although, the sexy threats he'd been texting to me over the past few days had weakened my resolve...and tempted me to continue ignoring him if he was truly going to follow through with them.

"Kinda goes hand in hand with being a lawyer, baby girl."

A delicious shiver raced up my spine at the endearment. And judging by the satisfied smirk on Eli's stupid, sexy face, he hadn't missed my reaction.

There was no point in hiding it any longer, so I asked, "If I give you another chance—the very last one you'll ever get from me—how will I know you won't stand me up again?"

"Let's go right now."

2

ASH

Nora blinked her big blue eyes at me, and I smiled, going for charming...but that was a stretch when you were a badass biker and a cutthroat lawyer. I could've turned on the silver-tongued, charismatic facade I used to enthrall a jury. But I wasn't gonna fake anything with Nora. The only way we'd work was with complete honesty. Otherwise, when the curtain that shielded finally lifted, she would be crushed under its weight.

"Now?" she asked, glancing up toward the ambulance cab where her partner was waiting. "I'm still on shift."

"When do you get off?"

She checked her watch, biting her lip. Unable to

stop myself, I used my thumb to free it, enjoying her tiny gasp and the heat in her eyes.

"Um...in about an hour."

Doubt clouded her face, and I wasn't about to give her the chance to change her mind. "Gonna follow you back to work and wait until you're done."

"You'll what?" She shook her head. "You don't have to—"

"Sure as fuck do, baby girl," I grunted, slipping my hand around her waist and slowly bringing her closer. "Need to make up for disappointing you."

She quickly dropped her gaze to my chest, but not before I saw the hope flare in her pretty blue orbs and the corner of her mouth kick up. "Are you sure?" Then her head swiveled to the right when the engine of a motorcycle roared to life. "On your bike?"

I cupped her chin and brought her face back to mine. "Nah. Got a truck. And you're worth the wait, baby girl."

"Okay," she whispered, her cheeks dusting with pink as she gave me a small smile.

"Truck is at my house, though," I told her reluctantly. "It's only a few minutes from here. Mind following me there first?"

Her eyes narrowed, and her nose wrinkled adorably. "Your house?"

"Yeah," I replied, confused as to why that bothered her.

"I guess it's convenient to live so close when you take women home."

I wanted to smile when I realized what was bothering her, but I had a feeling it would just make her mad. I wasn't gonna fuck up the second chance she was giving me. "Suppose it is," I answered, stamping down a grin when irritation flared in her eyes. "Never taken a woman to my house, though, so I never thought about it."

"Oh?" she chirped, looking much cheerier for a moment, then her expression fell again. "So you just hook up here at the clubhouse?"

I couldn't hold back my laughter anymore. "Adorable," I murmured with a shake of my head.

Nora glared at me. "I thought I told you—"

"Then stop being so fucking cute, and listen real good, baby girl." I drew her in until our bodies were pressed together. "Never been a hookup kind of guy."

"Oh?" she squeaked nervously, her cheeks blooming with red.

"Yeah, and while I do think you're adorable sometimes, I also think you're incredibly gorgeous." Lowering my head, I inhaled her scent of coffee and cinnamon. When our lips were only centimeters apart, I whispered, "And jealousy looks real fucking sexy on you, baby girl."

I didn't give her time to react before I pressed my lips to hers. Her tiny gasp gave me the opening I needed to slip my tongue into her mouth. She tasted like coffee and cinnamon, which were quickly becoming my favorite smell and flavor. I wondered if it was a drink she had a lot or if she was simply that sweet. I had a feeling it was the latter, and I couldn't wait to see if her pussy was just as delicious.

After a couple of minutes, I had to pull away before I lifted her by her round ass and took her to the nearest deserted room to find out.

"Damn. Could eat you for my next meal, but I need to make up for being a complete...blundering dunderhead?" I finished with a chuckle.

Nora shrugged, looking a little dazed, which made me feel smug satisfaction. "It seemed appropriate."

I laughed again, then released her but kept her hand in mine. "You good with stopping at my place, then?"

"That's fine unless we get a call. Then I'll have to meet you at the company station."

After giving her another quick kiss, I smiled. "Sounds like a plan."

Glancing around, I spotted two prospects staring at us with their mouths hanging open. Probably because they'd never seen me with a woman who was clearly more than a friend. Or it could've been because they'd rarely seen me smile unless I was talking to a jury.

"You." I pointed at the tall, gangly one. "Tell Prez I'm gonna push the meeting to tomorrow morning. And you"—I pointed at the shorter, even skinnier one—"go buy a bunch of pregnancy tests and give 'em to Wizard."

His face screwed up, and he muttered, "Seriously?"

My eyes narrowed, and my expression hardened. "You questioning my orders, probie?"

"No," he replied quickly. "Consider it done."

I nodded, and my face softened when I turned back to Nora. She was staring at me, her blue eyes clouded, but I wasn't sure what she was feeling.

"You okay?" I was a little worried that I'd scared her.

"Yeah...um...that was kind of..." Her skin flushed, her cheeks turning deep red, but she seemed to gather her courage before she blurted, "Hot."

I tossed my head back and laughed heartily, then pulled her in for another quick, hard kiss. "Glad you think so, baby girl. Now, let's go. Got some groveling to do so I can get some more of those sexy-as-fuck kisses."

A dreamy smile formed on Nora's gorgeous face. "I think you've earned a few," she said with a giggle.

"Good," I grunted as I turned her around and patted her tight ass to get her moving. "'Cause I'm already addicted."

Luck was on my side because they didn't get another call before Nora's shift ended. When she exited the building, she'd changed into a pink sundress that made her hair look even redder. Wasn't there some stupid rule about redheads wearing pink? Just another useless fact spouted by my mother, as if it would help me judge any woman I was considering marrying. *Well, Mother, to that I say bull-fucking-shit.* Nora looked like a goddess.

Her hair had been in a twist on the top of her head, but now it hung in soft waves down her back. I couldn't wait to feel those locks wrapped around my hands while I pumped my cock into her tight little pussy. I carefully adjusted myself before she caught sight of me, then gave her a slow, lazy smile.

"Lookin' gorgeous, baby girl."

"Thanks," she answered, a pink blush making her freckles pop. Eventually, I was gonna connect every last one with my tongue.

I took her hand and walked her the few steps to my truck, then helped her up inside. When I reached across her to clip in the seat belt, my arm brushed her tits, and her nipples poked through the fabric of her dress. Her quick intake of air made them jiggle a little, and I had to hold back a groan. Fuck...I was gonna end up needing her EMT services when I passed out from blue balls.

After making my way around the truck, I got in and settled in the driver's seat. There was a fancy little French restaurant around the corner, and I'd made a reservation as soon as she'd climbed back into her ambulance earlier.

It wasn't my style, but I would do whatever it took to convince Nora to give us a shot.

When I pulled into the parking lot, I glanced at her and was surprised to see her disappointed expression.

"Don't like French food, baby girl?"

"It's not that. It's just..."

I gently took hold of her chin and turned her head so she was looking right at me. "We can go wherever you want."

She licked her lips nervously, and I managed to hold back all the dirty thoughts it inspired and focus on my girl. "Really?"

"Anything you want."

"Could we...maybe go to a place that has really awesome burgers? And milkshakes?"

A wide grin split my face, and I nodded. "Got just the place, baby girl."

Ten minutes later, I drove up to The Fuel & Flame Diner. It was one of the legit businesses owned by the MC, while our main source of income walked the line between the laws of the land and our own brand of justice.

When someone needed to disappear, for whatever reason—as long as they weren't deserving of a beating or the business end of my gun—they came to us because we were the best at it. By referral only, of course.

Most of the patches had some type of skill that helped us forge the new identities and all the other shit that came along with wiping a life off the face of the earth. Obviously, I took care of the legal shit and the "illegal" legal shit. Along with my other duties, like making sure no one ended up in jail.

"I've driven by this place," Nora said happily. "But I've never gone in."

"Best burgers in town."

I hopped out of the truck and jogged around to open Nora's door and lift her to the ground. It was impossible not to steal a kiss from her pink rosebud mouth. Then I led her inside and lifted my chin at Rock, the patch who managed the diner.

"Anywhere," he informed me in his gruff, no-nonsense tone. He was a great guy, and his employees loved working for him, but he rivaled King with how much he scowled. I'd often wondered if he'd ever smiled at his longtime girlfriend, Deedee.

Several of my brothers, a few prospects, and some other random diners were scattered about the seating area, but a little corner seemed to offer more privacy, so I made a beeline for it.

After Nora slid into the booth, I followed her, grinning at her shocked expression.

"Not gonna pass up the opportunity to have you pressed against me." I winked, and my smile widened at her cute blush. "Doesn't hurt that you can't get away from me either."

Nora giggled and shook her head. "You'd be surprised. I'm limber and creative."

Fuuuuuck. She was gonna kill me.

I dipped my head and whispered, "Looking forward to learning more about that talent, baby girl.

'Fraid I'm gonna need an up close and personal demonstration to back up that claim."

Nora's blue eyes darkened with desire, and she licked her lips again, making it impossible for me to hold back a groan.

"Better order some food before I decide to eat you instead," I growled.

Nora swallowed hard, and I winked before sitting back up and handing her a menu.

Deedee appeared out of nowhere with a bright smile and a pad of paper. "Can I get y'all any drinks?" she asked in a Southern accent.

"How about a couple of Cokes, darlin'," I replied in my native Texan drawl.

Deedee's cheeks turned pink, and she shook her head. "Cokes it is. What kind?"

I glanced at Nora, and she chose a soda, then I asked for the same.

Deedee nodded, then smiled at Nora. "And who is this sweet young thing?"

I slipped my arm around Nora's waist and pulled her in close. "This is my Nora."

"Well, ain't she just pretty as a peach?"

"She's definitely got beauty to spare," I told her.

Nora's eyes bounced back and forth between us with something between awe and confusion.

But when her gaze locked with mine, my skin buzzed from the heat in the blue depths.

"This is Deedee," I introduced the older woman. "She's Rock's old lady." My chin bobbed toward the counter where he was working on receipts.

Turning back to the sweet woman I'd known since I was a prospect, I asked, "How's things your way?"

Deedee laughed. "Zeke's got his tail up. But what else is new?"

I tilted my head and glanced behind her at Rock, chuckling. "He's all hat and no cattle."

Her eyes twinkled. "Can't argue with that."

"He ain't got nothin' to fuss over. You're shinin' brighter than a diamond in a goat's ear."

Deedee's face reddened, and she giggled before looking at Nora. "Silver-tongued devil, ain't he? I swear, this boy could talk a cactus into blooming."

"I'm guessing I would agree with you if I knew what you were saying," Nora laughed. Then she looked between us again. "I know you're speaking English, but..."

I laughed and ignored when Deedee's eyebrows flew up and got lost in her hairline.

For fuck's sake, I wasn't *that* grumpy.

"Deedee is from Texas," I explained.

Nora canted her head and stared at me. "That explains her accent and interesting vernacular. What about you? That doesn't sound fake."

I shrugged. "Grew up in Texas. I can whip it out when I want to."

"Interesting." The heat was back in Nora's eyes, and I swallowed hard.

"How about two cheeseburgers with the works?" Thankfully, her question reminded me that we weren't alone because I'd been real damn close to losing control.

"Sounds good," I grunted, adjusting myself under the table, hoping to make things a little more comfortable in the groin. It didn't work. My shaft was so fucking big and hard, I wouldn't have been surprised if my long, thick cock burst through the zipper.

Deedee sauntered off, and I tried to think about anything that didn't involve a naked Nora.

"Not complaining, baby girl, but you gonna tell me why the long face at the French restaurant?"

Nora stiffened, then sighed. "It reminds me of my life, I guess."

Confused, I asked, "Your life?"

"Yeah. My parents...well, I grew up wealthy. My dad is the mayor of the town where we live. I spent my life in restaurants like that. Being the perfect daughter. Wearing the right clothes. Eating the appropriate food, with the correct silver." Her nose screwed up in disgust before she admitted, "I had a freaking 'coming out' party!"

I chuckled, and she threw me a death glare. "It probably sounds ridiculous to you, but—"

"Actually, I was laughing because I know how you feel."

"Pardon?" She blinked her big blue eyes, observing me with skepticism. "You had a coming out party?"

Snickering, I shook my head. "Cute, little smart-ass," I muttered. "Nah, but my father is a Texas senator. I was born with the proverbial silver spoon in my mouth. Or silver rattle."

One corner of my mouth lifted when she giggled.

"My parents would do just about anything to cement their 'family values' platform. Including having a kid."

Nora frowned and shook her head. "I'm sure they wanted—"

"Nope." I went on to tell her about my choices and how I ended up where I was. Happy and free.

"I didn't need more reasons to like you, Elias Prescott III."

"My full name? That's a surefire way to get a cherry-red ass, darlin'," I said, adopting my smooth Texas accent again.

Nora's cheeks turned pink, and she bit her bottom lip.

I inhaled deeply, then realized what a mistake it was when the scent of cinnamon and coffee hit my nose. "Need to get you home, baby girl," I grunted.

Disappointment flashed on her face before she gave me a fake smile.

Taking hold of her chin, I locked eyes with her. "Ending our date is the last thing I want to do. But I don't think you're ready for what would happen if I took you to my house."

Nora's lips curved into a sweet smile, and happiness twinkled in her bright blue orbs. "Oh," she replied softly. "I guess that makes sense."

With a frustrated growl, I slid out of the booth and grabbed her hand to pull her out and up beside me. Quickly, I retrieved my wallet from my back pocket and tossed some bills on the table.

The drive to her house was a new kind of torture, and I almost turned the truck around to take her home half a dozen times. But I'd messed up, and this was about proving how important she was to me beyond sex.

When I came to a stop in the circle drive of her house—a colonial, two-story brick house with a water fountain...yeah, a fucking water fountain in the center. I took in one last breath, savoring her smell. Then I cupped the back of her neck and brought her closer for a deep kiss that had my heart racing and my cock dripping with need.

"What time do you get done tomorrow?" I rasped.

"Um...three."

"Be ready for me to pick you up at six."

She beamed at me, then leaned in to give me a peck on the lips.

"That is not how you kiss your man, baby girl," I scolded. "But if I give you a demonstration, you won't make it outta this car. Stay here while I come get you."

I started to exit the truck when she laid her hand on my arm. "My parents are..." She sighed, looking frustrated and a little contrite. "I just need a little time to ease them into this."

I frowned but eventually relented. "I get it. Not gonna wait long, though."

"You won't have to."

I grunted in reply, then jumped out of my truck and jogged around to help her down from her seat.

"See you tomorrow, baby girl," I murmured before giving her a searing kiss, then patting her on the ass to get her moving.

Climbing back into my vehicle, I watched until she was inside before forcing myself to drive away.

3

NORA

"You're home late," my mother called as I shut the front door behind me.

Unfortunately, my parents' disapproval of my job didn't stop them from always sticking their nose into my business. More like the opposite since they didn't want me to mess up even more than I'd already done, as far as they were concerned.

My life would probably be much less stressful if I moved out, but I worried that it would ruin my relationship with them. Staying in my childhood home was just about the only decision I'd made since I turned eighteen that they actually agreed with. I wasn't quite ready to burn that bridge yet, but if they reacted negatively to Eli being in my life, that might be what pushed me to find a place of my own. We were just starting to get to know each other, but based on my strong reaction to him, I could easily see him quickly becoming an important part of my life.

Bracing myself for her reaction, I replied, "I went on a date after work."

"A date?" Mom shrieked.

I hadn't even finished hanging my bag in the front closet before she came running from the kitchen on the other side of the house, a miraculous feat considering the height of her heels. Even while home alone, she was dressed to the nines. Like always.

As she slid to a stop, I shook my head with a laugh. "Yes, Mom. A date... you know, the thing you've been trying to talk me into doing for years?"

"Only with someone eligible." She pressed her hand over her heart with an exaggerated gasp. "Preferably with a nice young gentleman who I set you up with. So many of my friends have sons who would be your perfect match. Unlike whomever you met while at that job of yours, I'm sure."

"I did meet Eli a couple of weeks ago while on a call," I conceded.

"Eli?" she echoed, tilting her head to the side. "That's actually quite a lovely name."

"It's short for Elias."

She gave a little shudder. "Nicknames are so passé."

If she knew what everyone else called him, she would be horrified, so I kept his road name—and his connection to a motorcycle club—to myself. "Well, his full name is quite a mouthful. Elias Prescott III."

Her eyes widened, and her gasp of delight was genuine this time. "Elias Prescott III...the senator's son who was in the news a couple of weeks ago because he'd disappeared from his social circle and popped back up again? And then promptly got shot by that awful woman before dropping out of sight again?"

"The one and only." I rolled my eyes. "With a name like that, who else could it be?"

"Who knew your job would actually land such a fantastic opportunity right in your lap?" She closed the distance between us and wrapped her arms around me for the first hug she'd given me in years. "My precious girl, I never should've doubted you. Well done."

If my mother knew me at all, she'd never think that I went out with Eli because of his family connections. But I had given up on her understanding how different we were long ago.

"Thanks, Mom," I whispered before stepping out

of her embrace to head upstairs to my room. She'd normally have more questions about my day—which really were just how she made little digs at what I'd chosen to do with my life—but the news of me dating a senator's son had thrown her off track.

As I padded into my bedroom and shut the door behind me, I couldn't help but wish that I had a different kind of relationship with my mother. One where I could tell her all about my first real date ever and have her gush over something besides Eli's parents. Unfortunately, that was never going to happen because we were too different.

She was the debutante who happily went along with my grandparents' plan to marry her off to my father, while I balked over the slightest suggestion of her setting me up with one of her friends' sons.

With the exception of my own "coming out party" when I turned sixteen, I had gotten out of attending any of the debutante balls by threatening to embarrass her in front of all of her hoity-toity friends. That was around the same time I signed up for the EMT track at my high school, so I told her I would wear blood-soaked scrubs to every event. Even if I had to fake the stains to make it happen.

Luckily, my father thought those parties were all nonsense, so he took my side, much to my mother's chagrin. Otherwise, he would have put his foot down, and I wouldn't have gotten out of them since his word ruled our house. Same with my grandfather and probably all of my great and great-greats, too.

I'd pushed against my father's rules as far back as I could remember. One of my mother's favorite stories to tell from my childhood was when I was two and planted my little hands on my hips while chanting "no" at him when he wanted me to eat broccoli with dinner.

She'd found it adorable, him not so much. What neither of them had bargained for was that my stubbornness would grow during my teenage years. Which was why I was so surprised by my reaction to the sexy threats Eli had sent me when I stopped taking his calls after our missed date.

I should've found them irritating. Or even infuriating. Instead, they sparked filthy fantasies about Eli every time I went to sleep.

After going on an actual date with him, I had a feeling they'd be more intense tonight. Especially after that kiss.

My lips curved into a dreamy smile as I headed into the bathroom to get ready for bed. When I finished up, I climbed on the mattress and clicked on my phone's screen to pull up the message thread with Eli and scrolled to when I first started to ignore his calls.

> **ELI**
>
> Pick up, baby girl. I get that you're pissed I had to cancel our date, but that doesn't mean we're over.

I had wanted to fire back with a text about how that was exactly what him backing out on our first date at the last minute meant, but I held off. It only got harder to stop myself from there.

The most recent messages had been the most difficult to ignore.

> **ELI**
>
> If you won't answer my calls, at least reply to one of my texts.
>
> **ELI**
>
> I'm not going to give up, baby girl. So you might as well talk to me before you've racked up so many spankings that you're perfect little ass will wear my handprint for days.

The thought of a guy giving me a spanking should've turned me all the way off...to the point where I blocked his number. But Eli's sexy threats only made me want to find out what his palm felt like against my butt.

As I stared down at the screen, contemplating how to reply without mentioning that particular topic when those messages were right there, three little dots appeared on the thread.

"Fiddlesticks," I breathed, hoping he hadn't seen the same thing when I accidentally hit the spacebar before scrolling up. That had been minutes ago, which meant he'd easily be able to guess how long I was obsessing over his darn threats.

I breathed a deep sigh of relief when his message came through.

> ELI
>
> Thanks for finally going out with me, baby girl. Meant it when I said I'd pick you up tomorrow.

My lips curved into a satisfied grin as my fingertips flew over the keyboard on my screen.

> ME
>
> Looking forward to it.

> ELI
>
> You like Italian? If so, I know the perfect place. Not fancy but fucking fantastic food.

I loved all kinds of pasta, so I licked my lips in anticipation.

> ME
>
> Sounds amazing! Now I'm even more excited for tomorrow night.

> ELI
>
> Is dinner all you're looking forward to?

I bit my bottom lip as I wondered how forward I should be. Deciding that my father was right about fortune favoring the bold, I went for it.

> ME
>
> And maybe some more of your kisses.

I waited with bated breath as those three little dots popped up, the eagerness building until his next message finally came through.

> ELI
>
> How about getting another date closer to me doling out the sweet punishment you earned for ignoring me?

My eyes widened at the question. I should've known Eli wasn't the kind of guy who'd let those sensual threats drop just because I'd accepted his apology for having to cancel our first date at the last minute. His boldness was probably a trait that made him a good lawyer...and was also one I found incredibly attractive. Even when I was angry with him.

But that didn't stop me from sending him a sassy reply.

ME

> Too bad none of the etiquette classes my mom forced on me had any rules about when that would be appropriate. You might be stuck waiting a lot longer than you think.

ELI

> Adding that to your tab, baby girl. Sweet dreams.

Another message popped up only a moment later.

ELI

> Of me.

Once again, my thoughts were all about Eli as I drifted off. But this time, I was filled with anticipation instead of frustration.

4

ASH

I eagerly reached for my phone when my text alert went off late the following morning. But instead of Nora, it was King reminding me about our rescheduled meeting.

"Dammit," I muttered. I'd been in the middle of an incredible dream starring Nora where I stared at my handprint on her sexy little ass while I fucked her from behind. Stiffly, I climbed out of bed and stomped into the bathroom for an arctic shower.

After grabbing a quick breakfast, I hopped on my hog and rode the short distance to the clubhouse.

Kevlar, Cross, and Shadow sat at the bar with Wizard standing behind it. Shadow—an enforcer and one of the best "cleaners" in the business—saw me first. He lifted his chin in greeting before shooting back his drink.

Wizard cocked his head and stared hard at me. "Don't look like a man who was up all night fucking," he said with a grin.

I narrowed my eyes and muttered, "Shut the fuck up, asshole. Not all of us are so hard up we have to go at warp speed."

Wizard snorted. "Don't pretend you haven't been celibate as long as I was before Thea."

He had a point. This MC was probably weird as shit to outsiders. Most of us older guys had gotten sick of the garbage that went along with dating or friends with benefits. The upside was that it meant our previous actions weren't gonna bite us in the ass if we finally met the right woman.

"You fuckers gonna stand there or get on with this meeting?" I growled, walking past them to the hallway that led to offices that belonged to King; Blaze, our vice president; Ace, our treasurer and money guy; Wizard; and me.

King was sitting behind his desk when I tapped on the doorjamb before entering at his nod. Blaze lifted his chin from where he was sprawled on a couch in a small sitting area. A large conference table was on the opposite side of the room, and two chairs sat directly in front of King's desk.

Echo and an enforcer, Cruze, came strolling in as I dropped onto a stuffed chair by Blaze while everyone else found a seat. Wizard sat at the table, then pulled his glasses from his pocket and slipped them on before setting up his laptop.

"Sent you all the dossier," he grunted as he typed on the keyboard. This meeting was about our newest prospective client. I'd been digging into his legal situation.

King tapped on his iPad, presumably to bring up the document.

"Read it last night," I muttered. "Lines up with my research, but there's more. This idiot is in deep shit. Drugs and hookers mostly. But no records of any violence or scamming."

"Neighbors didn't have anything bad to say about him," Echo chimed in. He'd been doing surveillance on the guy, watching him and nosing around to see what the people he interacted with thought of him. "Mostly kept to himself, but friendly if they spoke to him. Never saw the cops there. Basically, he was just a typical guy...forgettable even."

"Probably because he was an informant," I remarked.

Wizard and Echo's eyebrows shot to their hairline as they stared at me.

"No, he wasn't," Wizard disagreed vehemently.

"Yup," I replied, letting the P pop.

"Woulda found the records when I was digging into the legal shit for you," Wizard argued.

At the same time, Echo protested, "Woulda caught him talking to a cop."

I rolled my eyes. "Ever hear of the term 'off the books'? Means there's no record."

Wizard narrowed his eyes at me but huffed and started tapping on his keyboard with harder strokes than normal.

"It was lost in a bunch of useless, legal mumbo-jumbo. Codes and shit that would be hard for even a good lawyer to decipher. Lucky for the Hounds"—my expression turned smug—"I'm far better than fucking good."

Echo huffed, but I ignored his pouting.

"Charges against him aren't all bullshit, but some of them are obviously meant to be leverage. Gotten himself so deep that it wouldn't take more than a phone call to put him behind bars for a long stretch."

"Won't all that go away if we erase him?"

"Not when some of that leverage includes threats against his daughter."

"Daughter?" King growled. "He'd be leavin' his kid behind?"

Wizard looked like he was going to vomit. "He's got a kid?"

I decided not to mess with him. "Relax, man. It's in a sealed file, and he's not even on the original paperwork. He made a request for around thirty sealed adoption files a few years ago. Ostensibly, to help a client find a lost child."

The guy was a PI, or he played at being one anyway. He'd closed a case or two. But even a broken clock was right twice a day.

"There was no reason for you to go deep into his client files," I told Wizard with a shrug. "Only reason I found it was because he'd paid some halfwit lawyer to come up with a bullshit reason to get a court order for the DNA of one of the girls in one of those files. It was denied. But Wizard included the whole dossier when he sent me the legal files. I noticed that shortly after that debacle, he opened an account on a genealogy site."

"That's why you asked me to hack that account?" Wizard queried. "I couldn't figure out what the fuck you were looking for on there."

I nodded. "He'd had his DNA done. I noticed that he was watching another public 'tree,' and he had a suggestion from the site that he might be related to someone on there. When I realized the suggestion was a young girl whose birthday matched that other file, I started comparing life events. I was eighty percent sure he was trying to find his kid who'd been put up for adoption. After looking through the list of places he'd lived since she was born, I was convinced."

"Like you said, you're better than fucking good," Blaze said. "How the hell would the fuckers blackmailing him find the connection?"

"Just because I'm the best doesn't mean there aren't a few who are almost as good," I offered. "Anyway, there were references to his collateral in the paperwork, but I couldn't find a single asset, hidden or otherwise. There were a few other hints, so I connected the dots."

King rubbed his jaw thoughtfully. "If he goes to jail—"

"Or dies," Kevlar interjected.

King nodded. "Yeah. The daughter will be next in line to take on his shit?"

"Looks like it," I confirmed. "He wants the legal stuff wiped out so they have nothin' on her. Including scrubbing his DNA everywhere."

Cruze, one of the best thieves in the world, looked at me incredulously. "Everywhere?"

I nodded. "Everything that could lead back to him or his daughter. I'm talking about finding his childhood home and making sure we get rid of anything they might have kept."

"Seriously? Like they would have kept his baby toothbrush or something?" Cross suggested in a mocking tone, obviously of the opinion that it was a ridiculous idea.

"Baby teeth," Cruze suggested. "My mom kept all of mine."

Blaze nodded. "As fucked up as my situation was at home, I think my mom still has mine."

Echo's face skewed up in disgust. "That's some serial killer kind of shit…keeping people's teeth."

"Not 'people,' shithead," King grunted. "Parents and their kids. You'll understand when Violet has yours." After rolling his eyes, King turned his gaze back to me, clearly done with that conversation. "Is it possible?"

I sighed and rubbed a hand over my buzzed head. "Probably is the best I can give you right now."

"Same," added Wizard.

Shadow nodded. "Yeah. The circumstances aren't—"

There was a loud bang, cutting him off. Then someone shouted, "Where are your doctors? Get their asses here now!"

"Who the hell is ordering my men around?" King snarled as he jumped out of his chair and stalked to the front of the clubhouse.

I quickly followed, and when I got there, I muttered, "Fucking hell," as I rushed over to help.

Raffaele DeLuca, the head of the southern area of the DeLuca Crime Family, was holding one of Ink's arms while his lieutenant—and brother—Dacio, had a grip on his other. Ink was limping, favoring his right leg, which was bleeding profusely from a bullet hole in his upper thigh.

"Shit!" King roared. "Where the fuck is Razor or Flint?"

I pointed at a hallway across the lounge. "Medical site is at the end of the hall," I told them as I whipped out my phone and dialed Flint's number. "Son of a bitch," I snapped when it went to voicemail. "Where the fuck are you? Get your ass to the medical clinic ASAP." Then I hung up and tried Razor, but I knew he was on shift in the ER at the local hospital.

"No answer from either," I told Blaze, who had

caught up as I rushed after the men. King led the way while barking out orders.

Blaze shook his head. "Me either."

"What the fuck happened?" King roared at the brothers.

"Matteo è proprio un cagacazzo," Rafa snapped.

Ink raised an eyebrow at his cousin. *"Gielo dirai, stronzo?"*

"Tell me what?" King seethed.

Blaze's phone rang, and he answered immediately. "Where the fuck are you? Fucking hell. Ink's been shot. I don't know. Yeah. No, go and help Flint. Yeah. Call me when you're on your way."

"Motherfucker," he swore as he shoved his phone back into his pocket. "There was a fucking shoot-out on the south side of town. They're bringing in over twenty stupid punks, at least half are critical. They called Flint in to help."

"Don't Tomcat or Fallon have medical training from the Navy?" Rafa asked.

"Combat medicine maybe," King answered as he put gauze over the wound to stanch the bleeding. "But they spent most of their time in the air."

Rafa glanced at Dacio. "How long would it take to get Doc Franklin out here?"

Dacio shook his head. "He's got his hands full

with our injured men. I don't think he can get here any time soon."

"Well, somebody needs to fix my damn thigh!" Ink shouted, then groaned when the movement caused his leg to jerk. "Shit!"

"Let's check the damage level," I suggested, an idea forming. Rafa and I moved Ink as carefully as we could, turning him just enough for me to look over the back of his leg.

"Son of a bitch, that hurts!"

"Stop being such a baby," I grunted. "I was shot in the shoulder and didn't whine this much about it."

Ink shot me a scathing glare. "You had a damn flesh wound. A few inches higher, and I'd be singing soprano!"

Okay, he had me there. Still... "Flint had to dig the slug out, motherfucker," I muttered. "You can whine when he's got a scalpel playing hide-and-seek with a bullet."

Ink flinched, then groaned when we turned him back over.

"There's an exit wound, so he probably won't need surgery." I glanced at my watch and saw that it was after three. "I could call Nora," I proposed, looking at King.

He stared at me, thinking over my suggestion. This was club business...and apparently mafia-related. We didn't tell our women much about club business, but more importantly, Nora wasn't my old lady.

Yet.

"Do I need to have a vest sent out for stitching?" he asked, referring to the stash of female vests we kept on hand. We sent one out to have our name embroidered on the property patch when we were ready to give it to a woman.

"Absolutely," I answered immediately, without a shred of doubt in my voice.

King nodded. "Call her."

I pivoted on my heel to leave the room as I reached into my pocket for my phone again.

Nora picked up after a couple of rings. "Hi," she said softly.

Her voice washed over me, causing warmth to spread through my chest and streaks of lust to shoot to my groin.

I fucking hated that I was calling her to ask a favor. One that could blow up her plans for the future. But she was really our only option outside of the club or Rafa's organization.

"Hey, baby girl. Before I get to why I'm calling, I

want you to know that I've missed you all fucking day."

Nora sighed, her happiness at my admission clear in her tone. "You just saw me last night," she giggled.

"Yeah, a whole night and morning without seeing you, kissing you...I don't like it," I confessed. I was surprised at how easy that had been to say.

"I missed you, too."

"Which makes the favor I'm about to ask so much harder."

"Favor?"

"I wouldn't ask if I had any other choice at all. But Razor and Flint are stuck at the hospital, and the other doctor our...friends...use isn't available either."

"You need a doctor?" she clarified.

"We need the next best thing. That's you, baby girl."

"What happened?" Her voice was wary, and I winced before telling her the truth.

"One of my brothers took a bullet. He needs medical attention."

"A bullet?" she squeaked.

"The bullet went straight through, and he's stable, but the wound needs attention, and no one here has enough medical knowledge to make sure it's treated right so it heals properly and doesn't get infected. One of our doctors will be here as soon as they can, but it could be several hours."

"Um...I'll see what I can do."

"Are you sure?"

"Yes. It's one of your brothers. I want to help."

"Damn, you're amazing," I uttered. If I hadn't already been obsessed with her, I would have fallen hard and fast at that moment.

"So you've said," she sassed with a giggle.

Chuckling, I teased, "You just might work off a few of those spankings I owe you."

"Um...I..."

A laugh rumbled in my chest as I knocked on the doorframe and gave King a thumbs-up. "I'll be there as fast as I can, baby girl," I told her and headed to the garage where I'd parked my bike.

5

NORA

I never thought I'd agree to treat a bullet wound that couldn't be reported to the police, but I hadn't hesitated to grant Eli's favor. Not when his club brother's life was at stake.

I didn't really think about what I was about to do until I was back downstairs twenty minutes later, headed toward the door with my first-aid kit in one hand and my cell in the other.

"You just got home from work. Where are you going?" my mother asked.

I shifted my position, hoping it would make it more difficult to see the kit. "Eli is picking me up earlier than planned."

Her nose wrinkled as her gaze darted down my body. "You're wearing that for your date?"

Hearing the rumble of what I was hoping was his motorcycle, I replied, "Yup," and slipped out the door.

Unfortunately, my mother wasn't going to let me get away that easily. She followed me outside, where her wide smile of greeting quickly slipped from her face when she saw Eli. Straddling his bike in black boots, jeans, a black T-shirt, and his leather vest, he looked nothing like the lawyer she'd been expecting.

"Nora Elizabeth Stoll, you get back here right this instant," she demanded.

"Sorry, Mom. No can do," I called back as I handed Eli the first-aid kit to tuck into his saddlebag. Then I popped the helmet he shoved at me onto my head and climbed onto the motorcycle behind him.

I'd never been on one before, but being wrapped around his muscular body made me an instant fan. I also appreciated how quickly we drove off because my mom hadn't stopped yelling since she realized I was actually leaving with him. I wasn't looking forward to dealing with her, but I had a bigger problem to deal with first—treating a bullet wound.

With my upbringing, I wasn't very familiar with motorcycle clubs, but I knew enough that I wasn't surprised the Hounds of Hellfire didn't want the cops notified about a bullet hole in one of their members. The situation when I met Eli was different because the woman who shot him was the head of some con ring who had targeted him, judging from what the media said about the whole thing afterward. How that woman had thought Eli would be an easy mark baffled me, but I didn't expect to ever learn what truly happened.

Either way, that must not have been the type of business that could get Eli's club into trouble. If he called me for help, this must be. I wasn't exactly the best choice, considering I was an EMT who was studying to be a paramedic and had limited experience with things like bullet wounds, other than stopping the bleeding and getting the patient to a hospital.

Luckily, Mark had been a combat medic. He'd taught me all kinds of stuff typical paramedic training wouldn't go anywhere near. My biggest concern was if the bullet was still in the guy...I'd have to insist they go to a hospital because they needed a surgeon to dig it out.

However, despite my internal struggle, I didn't want Eli to think he couldn't count on me. So I squared my shoulders and put a confident expression on my face.

"I'm guessing it's safe to assume that you're not

going to be able to answer any of my questions even though my medical training has gotten me pulled into club business?" I asked after he parked his motorcycle in front of the clubhouse.

He flashed me an apologetic smile and shook his head. "Sorry, baby girl. There's always gonna be stuff I can't share with you, including the rare times when you have the right to be curious about what's going on."

Climbing off the bike, I heaved a deep sigh. "That's what I figured you'd say."

He waited until he grabbed my first-aid kit from the saddlebag to ask, "You gonna be able to live with that?"

"I wouldn't be here if I didn't think I could handle it."

Some of the tension eased from his shoulders at my answer, but any concern that either of us had about how club business might impact our relationship was shoved on the back burner while I followed him inside.

"Where's my patient?" I asked the first guy I saw.

He jerked his chin toward the hallway on the far-left side of the large room and answered, "In the medical clinic."

"Medical clinic?" I echoed once we were out of earshot of his club brothers.

Eli interlaced our fingers while he led me past several doors. "Two of the guys are doctors, Razor and Flint. They made sure that we were equipped to handle any kind of medical emergency."

"And yet, here I am about to take care of a freaking bullet wound for you," I muttered, wondering why I was surprised that their ranks included a couple of doctors when Eli was a lawyer.

"I'm sorry I had to ask you to risk your career for me, baby girl." He squeezed my hand. "Couldn't pull either of them out of the hospital fast enough to take care of Ink. I swear, I won't make a habit of this."

As he reached for the knob on the door at the end of the hallway, I tugged on his other hand so he looked at me over his shoulder. "I might give you crap for making the call, but if you're ever in a similar situation again, I expect you to do exactly that. My job is nothing compared to someone's life."

"Fucking hell," he growled before turning toward me. Cupping my cheeks with his large hands, he tilted my head back to claim my mouth in a passionate kiss that took my breath away.

Unfortunately, it ended too soon...when Echo

flung open the door behind him and grunted, "Do that shit on your own time. Ink needs her help now."

"Sorry," I mumbled, my cheeks filling with heat.

"You got nothing to apologize for," he reassured me, jerking his chin toward Eli. "He's the one I was dishing that shit out to."

"Damn well better have been me," Eli retorted, pressing against my lower back with his palm to guide me into the room filled with equipment any clinic would envy. "She's risking herself to help us out."

"I sure as fuck appreciate it," the man sprawled on the exam table rumbled. "Really don't want any of you to have to tell my *mamma* that I got shot, let alone died."

"Nobody is dying here today," I reassured him, rushing over to the sink to wash my hands before tugging on a pair of gloves. Then I began my examination of him.

"I'm Ink, by the way," he said through gritted teeth while trying to smile. "Figured you ought to know if you're gonna be getting up close and personal with my body."

"You got a death wish, Ink?" Eli snarled.

"No, sir," he replied immediately.

"Then keep your fucking mouth shut and your eyes and hands away from my woman."

I held back a smile at Eli's display of jealousy. It probably should have bothered me...but it was so hot.

"Nora," I told Ink.

First, I assessed his airway, breathing, and circulation while applying pressure to the wound in his thigh, which already had a square of gauze covering it. Once I confirmed his ABCs were good, I murmured, "Your pulse and blood pressure are a little high, but that's to be expected when you've been shot."

"Hurts like a motherfucker," he admitted.

"I'm sure." Turning to Eli, I asked, "Can you apply pressure to the wound while I perform a brief neurological assessment?"

"Sure," he quickly agreed, gently placing his palm over mine and giving Ink a giant smile.

When I slid my hand away from Ink's thigh, he pressed down. Ink groaned in pain. "Shit, man. Do you have to push down so fucking hard?"

"Yes, he does," I replied, retrieving my penlight from my bag to stimulate his pupils.

Ink shot a dubious look at Eli but didn't protest again.

The direct and consensual responses were good, so I quickly swung the light back and forth between his eyes to check his pupillary responses. "There doesn't seem to be any issues with the optic nerve, and your pupils are equal in size without being abnormally dilated or constricted."

"That good?" Ink asked.

"Yup," I confirmed with a nod, tucking the penlight back into my bag. "Just need to check your temperature, and then I can get to work on that gunshot."

After I confirmed he didn't have a fever, I gestured for Eli to lift his hand. Peeling the gauze away from Ink's skin, I peered at the entry wound. "The good news is that you were shot in the lateral aspect of the thigh."

"Why's that good?" Ink asked.

"The muscle mass is thick enough to allow a bullet to pass through without hitting major blood vessels or bone," I explained as I prodded at the edges to test how much blood seeped out. I was relieved to see that the bleeding was controlled. "But it depends on the bullet's trajectory, so I'm gonna need to take a look at the other side of your leg to make sure there's an exit wound and see where it is."

"That makes sense, but I gotta admit that getting up here wasn't as easy as I made it look."

At Ink's confession, Eli and Echo moved to either side of the exam table and helped him roll onto his side. I nudged the hem of his athletic shorts up a little to get a better look at the exit wound. "Looks as though your muscle tissue provided a path for the bullet to travel without coming out this side too quickly."

"I woulda thought the faster, the better," Echo muttered.

I continued to prod at Ink's wound while I explained, "It seems counterintuitive, but the faster the bullet goes through your body, the more damage it does along the way. The higher kinetic energy creates larger tissue displacement."

Ink hissed in pain at my delicate exploration of the hole where the bullet exited his body. "I'm just glad I have an exit wound, unlike when Ash got shot. I'd hate for you to be stuck digging the bullet out like Razor did for him."

My head jerked up, and I glared at Eli. "I knew you were trying to hide that there wasn't an exit wound that day, you big lummox."

Shrugging, he didn't look the least bit embarrassed to have been caught. "Sure was."

"I know you have two club brothers who are doctors, and it's been weeks since you were shot, but I'm going to want to take a look at your shoulder to see for myself that you're okay since you didn't let me do my job properly in the first place."

"No need to get sassy, baby girl." He winked at me. "Just say the word, and I'll strip down for you whenever you want."

"Quit flirting with the girl and let her fix me up," Ink growled.

Eli glared at him, and I muttered, "Sorry."

I gathered the supplies I needed to clean and pack the wound. Once that was done, I announced, "You're going to need stitches, but not until the initial swelling goes down. If one of the club doctors can't do it for you, you'll be forced to go to the hospital. My training only gets us so far."

"Thanks, but I'm sure Razor or Flint will handle it," Ink assured me as I strode over to the sink.

After pulling off my gloves, I washed my hands again while Echo and Eli helped Ink off the exam table. Then Echo guided Ink out of the room, leaving Eli and me alone.

He brushed his lips against my cheek and murmured, "Thank you."

"I think you can show me your gratitude better than that."

I was aiming for a kiss because I couldn't get the one he'd given me after our date out of my head, but I got more than I was bargaining for.

6

ASH

I wanted to kiss Nora so fucking badly that my mouth was watering at the thought. But my cock was throbbing, and my mind was rapidly clearing of any thoughts except getting her naked. Which meant we needed to be alone right the fuck now.

"Come with me, baby girl," I said quietly as I grabbed her hand and quickly led her down the hall to the recreation area.

A few guys were scattered around and asked about Ink, but I ignored them, going straight to the stairs that led up to the rooms on the second floor. Even though I lived in a house not far from the compound, being an officer had several privileges, like a permanent room with an en suite bathroom. I only used it when I worked so late that I didn't feel like going home or when I needed to be on call for something.

Some of the others lived on-site, and there were open rooms for anyone who needed to crash here, but the reserved rooms were for officers and enforcers.

"Where are we going?" Nora asked breathlessly.

"To be alone," I growled. At the top of the stairs, I turned right and went down three doors before stopping and digging a key out of my pocket. Once I got it unlocked, I turned the knob and placed my hand on Nora's belly, gently pushing her backward until we were far enough in to slam the door shut behind me.

"So you can show me your gratitude?" she asked breathlessly.

"Abso-fucking-lutely. Also think it's about time I doled out that punishment you've been racking up."

Nora's blue eyes widened and filled with shock and curiosity. "You-you're-you're going to um..."

I grinned wickedly. "Redden your pretty little ass until you can't sit down tomorrow?"

Her mouth formed a cute little O, and I slowly guided her back until her legs hit the edge of the bed.

"We'll get to that, baby girl. First, I'm gonna

thank you for being so damn amazing today." I shook my head and clarified, "Every fucking day."

My hands spanned her waist, and I yanked her against my body as my mouth crashed down onto hers.

"You taste so fucking good," I groaned against her lips before sinking into a deep, drugging kiss. My hands glided down and around to palm her delectable ass, hoisting her up so her legs wrapped around my waist. Then I fell forward so she was lying on her back with my body blanketing hers.

Our position had my cock firmly cuddled into the apex of her thighs, and I rocked gently, ripping my lips away and burying my face in her neck when she moaned.

"Those sexy little sounds are gonna break me, baby girl," I rasped, sucking in a deep breath and trying to hold on to my control.

"That sounds promising," she giggled.

My lips captured hers again, and I tried to go slow as I peeled away her clothes. But with every inch of bared skin, my cock throbbed harder and my body craved to be inside her.

When she was naked, I stood back, and my eyes swept over her, admiring her pale skin that made her freckles stand out. My tongue itches to trace each one, and I promised myself to do just that another time. I only had so much sanity, and it was gonna take all of it to spank her pretty little ass before popping her cherry.

"Baby girl?"

"Umm...yeah?" Nora lifted her head, watching me with a confused expression.

I bent over and caged her in with my arms on both sides of her. "Are you a virgin?"

She bit her lip and nodded her head, her blue orbs suddenly filled with worry.

I smiled to put her at ease. "Gotta admit, that makes me really fucking happy."

Color bloomed on her cheeks. "It does?"

"I woulda wanted you no matter what, baby girl. But being the only man to be inside you is bringing out the cavemen in me," I told her with a wink.

"Caveman?"

Grinning, I slowly slid down her body. "Yeah. I'm obsessed, jealous, and ready to fucking kill any man who looks at my woman. Just like a caveman."

Nora giggled, but it quickly trailed off when I pushed her legs open.

Kneeling between her legs, I took in the sight of Nora's bare, dripping pussy. My breath got caught in my lungs. Holy fucking shit. I'd never in my life seen anything so beautiful and mouthwatering.

Dropping onto my stomach, I parted her pussy lips with my thumbs and leaned in, inhaling deeply before finally licking up her center.

Fuck, yes, I thought with a low groan. I finally had my mouth on my woman, and her pussy was even sweeter than I'd imagined.

I skimmed a single digit up through her slit, and when it came away covered in her arousal, I licked it clean with a grunt of pleasure.

"You taste so fucking incredible, baby," I groaned as I dove in to drink her nectar straight from the source.

Nora cried out when I blew over her bundle of nerves, then sucked hard before biting down lightly.

I licked a few times more, enjoying her little wiggles as pleasure invaded her body. When I pushed my tongue into her tight channel, Nora gasped, and her juices gushed into my mouth.

Raising my head, I met her hazy eyes and licked my lips. "Am I showing you enough appreciation, baby girl?" I teased.

Nora's blue eyes were wide as she stared back at me, leaning up on her elbows with her long red hair spilling over her shoulders and playing peekaboo with her stiff, rosy nipples.

"Feel free to thank me anytime," she panted, making me chuckle.

"Adorable."

Nora's nose scrunched. "Seriously? When I'm naked and you're licking my...um..."

"Pussy?" I supplied with a smirk.

"Yes, that. I am not adorable! I'm a...a..." She looked frustrated.

"A sexy-as-fuck woman?"

She nodded firmly.

"A little vixen who's been taunting me with the promise of spanking her ass?"

Nora gasped. "I have not! I—"

Her eyes rolled back in her head, and she moaned when I covered her center with my mouth again.

Her moans were the sweetest sound, going straight to my big, aching dick.

Following through with my promise, I ate her pussy until she was shaking with ecstasy, her hands fisted in the sheets as she cried out.

It was the most beautiful thing I'd ever seen, but I wanted more. I shed my clothes and climbed over her, lowering myself until no space remained between us.

My mouth covered hers, and I explored her mouth, our tongues rubbing together as we drank from each other's lips. I angled my head for deeper access, and her tits rubbed against me as her breathing picked up. Her taut nipples poked my chest, and I glided my hands up from her hips to cup the soft, round globes. She moaned when I gently squeezed them and brushed my thumbs over the hard peaks.

I loved how fucking responsive she was, her nipples tightening even more as I played with them, her body pressing against mine as though she couldn't get close enough, and her tongue dancing and twisting seamlessly with mine.

She tested my control, but I wasn't gonna fuck her until I'd left my mark. Tearing my mouth away, I smiled wickedly. "Now that I've thanked you properly, it's time for the spankings you earned, baby girl."

Nora's mouth formed a little O, and her face registered shock. "You're actually going to spank me?" she squeaked.

"Don't say anything I don't mean, Nora," I

informed her in all seriousness. "Now turn over and put that pretty little ass in the air."

Her eyes darkened with desire, and though she still looked a little hesitant, she did as she was told.

Looking at her soft, unmarked skin, I was grateful I'd shed my pants. Otherwise, my cock probably would have ripped right through them in a desperate effort to get to her.

I raised a hand, and as I brought it down on her pale cheek, my cock jerked, releasing a spurt of precome. When I slapped the opposite side, it left a pink print that nearly caused me to come right then.

"Fuck, that looks good on you, baby girl," I grunted.

Nora let out a small sound, so quiet I almost missed it. So I spanked each cheek again, and my body caught fire when she cried out.

I slipped a hand between her legs and drew a finger through her slit. "Fucking drenched," I muttered.

When I raised my arm, her juices were dripping down my hand. I popped a finger in my mouth and groaned as I licked the digit clean. Coffee and cinnamon. I was suddenly starving, but I wasn't done giving my girl her punishment.

I kept spanking her luscious ass, stopping after

each few to drag a finger through her pussy for another taste of her sweet cream. The harder I brought my hand down, the more liquid gushed from her center.

Eventually, the pink handprint I'd left on each ass cheek stopped fading. I smiled wickedly, thinking about how she'd be reminded of her punishment every time she sat down the next day.

But I wanted her to feel me inside her every time she moved.

I flipped her over and sucked each of her sweet nipples before gently pushing her shoulders so she was lying flat on her back.

With a low growl, I slid my cock between her slick folds and groaned as the heat of her pussy wrapped around me.

The feeling was so intense that I suddenly realized I wasn't wearing protection. But the thought of taking her with something between us went out as fast as it came in. I wanted to be inside her bare...and if she got pregnant, even better.

"You on anything, baby girl?" I rasped.

Her eyes widened, and she shook her head. "Fiddlesticks! Do you have a condom?"

I shook my head. "Nope. Not gonna use one either." My tone made it clear this wasn't up for discussion. I pushed in an inch more, and her eyes closed as she moaned. "Popping this sweet little cherry bare."

"But—" She gasped when I pulled her legs around my waist and pushed in until I bumped into the proof of her virginity.

I was having a hell of a time holding back, but I hated that I had to cause her any kind of pain. I touched my forehead to hers and apologized, "I'm so sorry I have to hurt you, baby girl."

She looked up at me with a little fear, but I was proud as fuck of her when she drew up her courage and nodded, placing her hands on my face. "I know," she said tenderly. "But I want this more than anything, Eli. Please, make me yours."

"You're already mine," I growled before taking hold of her hips and surging forward until I was balls deep in her virgin pussy. "Fuck!" I bellowed, completely shaken by the ecstasy that washed over my body.

It took everything in me not to come as I stilled to give her time to adjust to me.

Tears leaked from the edges of her eyes, and I brushed them away with my thumbs before kissing each one as I waited for her to stretch and accommodate my big, fat cock.

Soon, I felt her begin to relax and take a deep breath.

I brushed a soft kiss over her lips as I circled my hips, testing her level of pain. She moaned into my mouth, and her legs tightened around me.

"Ready for more, baby girl?" I practically begged through clenched teeth.

"I think so," she answered hesitantly.

I pulled almost all of the way out before slamming back in. Nora threw her head back and shouted as her walls clamped down on me like a vise.

"Holy shit," I groaned. "You feel amazing. And fuck, knowing I popped your sweet cherry, that this pussy will only ever know my cock, is making it really fucking hard not to lose control."

I picked up a steady rhythm, fighting the grip her pussy had on my dick. "Eli," she cried out, her head thrashing from side to side, and her nails digging into my biceps.

"Fucking love hearing my name on your lips, baby girl," I growled.

Tingling started at the base of my spine, and my balls drew up, feeling heavy and full.

"Not gonna last much longer," I warned as I picked up the pace, fucking her fast and hard while a little come oozed from my shaft with every thrust. I wouldn't give in until she was in the throes of an orgasm so that she felt intense bliss more than pain.

I punched my fists into the mattress and shifted. The new angle sent me even deeper with the next thrust, and Nora's whole body shuddered. "Oh yes! Eli! Yes!"

Rising to my knees, I watched my cock disappear and reappear coated in her sticky cream.

"I need you to come, Nora," I gritted through clenched teeth. "Now."

Nora screamed with every slam of my hips, hovering on the edge. So I used the pad of my thumb to rub circles on her clit.

"Eli!" she whined desperately. "I'm so...oh yes!"

I pulled out and slapped her pussy before slamming back in. Nora tensed right before her breath caught, then a second later, she screamed my name as she flew apart.

"Fuck!" I shouted as I planted myself as deep as possible when my orgasm shot down my spine and exploded out of my cock. Her pussy milked my shaft in strong pulses, sucking the jets of come up into her womb.

"That's it, baby girl," I groaned. "Squeeze me. Oh, fuck yeah."

I continued to thrust, dragging out her orgasm

until she begged me to let her rest. When my climax began to taper off, I was sapped of my strength and almost collapsed on top of her. I didn't want to crush her, so I cuddled her close as I rolled over. Content, I drifted to sleep still buried deep inside her.

7

NORA

During all those days when I was fighting my attraction to Eli, I never let myself believe that I would find myself here—in his bed, with his muscular body wrapped around mine...after he had taken my virginity. If I had, I wouldn't have been able to resist him, and this would have happened much sooner.

But I wasn't going to dwell on the extra time we could've had together. In the grand scheme of things, a couple of weeks wasn't worth beating myself up over. Especially when I had been standing up for myself and what I wanted in a relationship.

Instead, I was going to focus on where we were at now. Which was a really freaking good place.

Twisting in his embrace, I took a moment to

appreciate how his expression softened in sleep. Eli was an intense guy and thirteen years older than me, but something was boyish about him when he was vulnerable like this. His long lashes rested against his cheeks, and his kissable lips were slightly parted as puffs of air blew through them.

I would've happily stared at him while he slept—like a creepy fangirl—for longer than I wanted to admit, except his eyes opened. There was no haziness in his eyes. It was just my luck that he was more alert than anyone should be upon first waking.

"Good morning," I murmured, my cheeks filling with heat at being caught gawking at him while he slept.

Luckily, Eli didn't seem to mind. His palm pressed against my lower back, bringing me flush against his body. "That's not how you say good morning to your man, baby girl."

"It isn't?" I asked, lifting my hand to rake my fingernails over the buzzed hair at the back of his head.

"Not even close."

That was all the warning I got before he claimed my mouth in a deep kiss. Any worry I had about not brushing my teeth yet was lost to the passion that quickly built between us. There was a dull throb in my core from him taking me last night, but that did nothing to tamp down the desire I felt.

When he finally ended the kiss, I let out a little whimper of protest. His lips curved into a smirk before he rasped, "Gonna take that sweet sound you just made as confirmation that you agree with how we should say good morning to each other from now on."

There was no point in denying it when I was pressing my thighs together to ease the ache between them that his kiss had created. "You sure can."

"That's my good baby girl."

I shivered at the praise, and his smirk widened at my reaction. Narrowing my eyes, I dug my nails into his shoulders. "You need to be careful with that voice of yours. It should be classified as a lethal weapon."

"I'll keep that in mind." He brushed his lips against mine again. "And use it more often if that's the kind of reaction I get outta you."

I wasn't surprised by his response since he was the kind of guy to use every tool at his disposal. Something he'd had to learn when he broke away from his family—which I respected. And I appreciated that he always had the perfect comeback when I verbally poked at him. Intelligence was definitely a turn-on for me. "Good, my evil plan worked then."

"You're gonna keep me on my toes, aren't you?" he asked, stroking his palm down my side to cup my butt through the sheet covering me.

"Hopefully." I waggled my brows. "I have a feeling it's the only way to keep you in line."

Brushing light kisses across my jawline and down my neck to my pulse point, he murmured, "You sure that's what you really want, baby girl?"

"Nope, definitely not." I tilted my head to the side to give him better access, and his deep chuckle sent a sensual shiver down my spine.

"That's what I thought." He brushed my hair to the side to kiss down my shoulder, giving my butt a gentle squeeze. "Just like I'm hoping you earn yourself more punishments in the future because I discovered last night that I fucking love the sight of my handprint on your perfect ass."

I wasn't sure what had surprised me more...that his spanking had turned me on or that I'd let him take me without anything between us. I couldn't imagine that many virgins did something like their first time having sex. And as a medical professional, I knew the risks I'd been taking when I hadn't insisted on Eli wearing a condom. But none of that had mattered to me in the heat of the moment, and I was less worried about it this morning than I probably should be.

Even after the bad first impression Eli had made—and the hurt he'd caused when he'd had to cancel our date—I trusted him. It was just that simple.

Beaming a mischievous smile his way, I teased, "With how stubborn I can be, I'm fairly confident that'll happen sooner than I might like."

His fingertips traced the curve of my butt. "I'll keep a tally until you're fully recovered."

"Aw, gee...thanks." I rolled my eyes. "That's so sweet of you."

He shook his head with a chuckle. "Not sure anyone's ever called me sweet, even when they were being sarcastic."

"Oooh, another first for us."

This time, he rolled his eyes, making me giggle. Unfortunately, our little bubble was burst by the ringing of his cell. Twisting around, he snagged the phone from the bedside table and glanced at the screen. "Sorry, gotta take this."

"Go ahead." I pressed a quick kiss against his shoulder before crawling off the bed, grabbing his discarded shirt from last night to tug it over my head. "I need to use the bathroom anyway."

"There should be an extra toothbrush under the sink if you want it."

Remembering what he'd told me about not being into hookups, I glared at him over my shoulder. "Oh really?"

He flashed me a knowing grin. "Relax, killer. It's only because the kind I like are easier to find in two packs."

"Good."

His answering laughter only lasted a moment before I heard him say, "Hello."

After using the toilet and washing my hands and face, I discovered he'd been right about the toothbrush. Sadly, I discovered he'd also been right about needing to take that call when I was done.

Eli was perched on the edge of the mattress, waiting for me with a disappointed expression. "C'mere, baby girl."

I padded over to stand between his legs. "What's wrong?"

"I know I said I didn't have anywhere I needed to be today, but it turns out I have to head to court."

I puffed out my bottom lip in an exaggerated pout. "I was looking forward to spending the day with you. It was the best part of having a couple of days off in a row."

"Me too, baby girl." He brushed his lips against mine in a quick kiss. "But this isn't the kind of request I can turn down."

I understood what it was like when duty called, so I wasn't going to give him too hard of a time. "Rain check?"

"As many as you want. My free time is yours."

"There you go, being a silver-tongued devil again." I stroked his bearded cheek, the bristles scraping my palm. "I'm going to have to work hard to hold my own with you."

His hazel eyes were filled with mirth as he replied, "You more than kept up with me last night."

I swatted at his bare chest, laughing softly. "You know that's not what I meant."

"True," he conceded. "But that doesn't make it any less funny."

"You better get going or you're going to be late for court."

"Then quit making it so damn hard." He climbed off the mattress and gestured at his erection. "Literally and figuratively."

My giggles dried up as I watched him dress in a three-piece suit that had to have been custom-made for his muscular body. As amazing as he looked naked, he was somehow even sexier when he dressed in his designer armor for court. It made me want to jump his bones, but I kept my reaction to myself so that I didn't really end up making him late.

He grabbed something from his closet and tossed it onto the bed, then came to stand in front of me. After bending down and kissing me senseless, he jerked his chin to what turned out to be his cut. "Wear that today."

"Why?" I asked curiously. Wasn't it a big deal for MC guys to have a woman wear their vest?

"So everyone knows you're mine."

He kissed me one more time, then reluctantly walked away.

The sight of him walking out the door was just as good, so I fanned myself with my hand before getting up to start my day. One that would be much less fun since I couldn't spend it with Eli.

8

ASH

I loved being a lawyer. I'd known it was my calling since I was ten and watched a show that starred a lawyer, and in the episode, he was in court. He'd wiped the floor with the prosecution and charmed the jury—had them practically eating out of the palm of his hand.

It might also have helped that the man being prosecuted was a corrupt politician.

I'd never regretted my decision until the moment I had to leave Nora when we could've spent the day in bed. Naked.

King and Blaze were in my office when I stomped inside, scowling.

"Sorry to take you away from your woman." Blaze's apology was clear in his voice. He was married and as obsessed with his wife as I was with Nora, so I knew he understood how shitty this situation was.

I nodded and held my hand out for the files he was holding. Taking them with me, I sat in the chair behind my desk and began to scan them.

"Where is Francesca?" I asked, referring to Francesca DeSantis, the lead lawyer on the legal team that handled their mafia shit.

"Her grandfather is sick," Blaze explained. "They're pretty sure this is it, so she went back to North Carolina."

It was hard to be pissed at her when she was taking care of her family. But I could still be plenty mad at Rafa.

"And the rest of the fucking army of lawyers they have working for them?" After just reading through a few pages, I knew the answer but asked the question anyway.

"This was top priority. They didn't trust anyone but Francesca to handle it."

I nodded and kept flipping pages, familiarizing myself with the case. Francesca had been valedictorian at Yale for her undergrad and graduated *summa cum laude* from Harvard Law. Her GPA had been almost as high as mine when I'd graduated.

Considering I was stepping in to fill her shoes at the last minute, it was also a good thing I had one more step up on her. I had an eidetic memory.

"Rafa will meet you at the courthouse with the client two hours before court so you can talk with him," King instructed.

I took a little more time to familiarize myself with the case details, then packed a briefcase and headed out. Since I'd ridden my bike, I needed a ride back to my house to grab my car—the Mercedes I drove when I had business at the courthouse.

Cross was coming out of the kitchen as I entered the lounge. Perfect.

He always had at least one of the cars he was restoring in the garage at the clubhouse. "Yo. You got a working car here?"

"It runs," he replied with a chuckle.

"I need a ride back to my house."

"Sure."

I suddenly remembered that my woman hadn't picked up her car yet. We'd used my truck for our date, and she hadn't been back to work before I called her to help with Ink. Her plan had been for her partner to drive her in for her next shift, but that didn't help with getting her home now. "Thanks.

And can you have a couple of prospects grab Nora's car from work and bring it here?"

"Can do."

Cross had always been a man of few words, so I didn't expect anything more.

After picking up my Mercedes, I drove to the courthouse well before Rafa and my client arrived.

I went through the process to get inside, then went to one of the small conference rooms to wait. When I was inside the quiet space, I dialed Francesca's number.

"*Grazie a Dio per te,*" Francesca sighed when she answered. "I owe you, Ash."

"Big time," I agreed.

"*Stronzate,*" she muttered, calling bullshit. "Like I haven't covered for your ass before."

"On a case this big? Nah."

"Okay, I'll give you that. This is the boss's godson, and I don't fancy being the next body floating in the East River."

"So you put that on me, huh?"

Francesca laughed. "Oh, shut up, big shot. I gave you everything you need to wrap this up with a neat little bow on it. Assuming you're still as good at handling a jury as you used to be."

I scoffed. "Even if I had lost my touch, I'd still kick your ass in the courtroom, kid."

"If you want to believe that, fine. Whatever it takes to get you to win this case."

"Tell me what the file doesn't," I requested as I took a seat and put my feet up on the table.

After an hour, I was even more impressed than when I'd read the brief and notes for her strategy that she'd left for me.

"Excellent plan, Francesca."

"Thanks. Now go execute it like the badass lawyer you are."

"Done," I replied before hanging up.

The defendant had been charged with possession of stolen property and conspiracy. What Francesca and I "didn't" know was that the charges weren't completely without merit. The southern branch of the DeLuca Crime Family focused primarily on smuggling art and antiquities.

The property in question was a shipment coming off a freighter from Italy. Bronson had been there to take possession of it, but the police had rolled in after the smugglers left and before Bronson had even laid a finger on the stolen artifacts.

They'd arrested him, and over the course of the trial, they'd nearly convinced the jury of his guilt.

They'd skirted around illegal search and seizure by the skin of their teeth, keeping the case from being thrown out before it even began.

The prosecutor was a surprisingly good one, and he'd kept the jury from falling for Francesca's attempts to insinuate that they fabricated evidence and had unreliable witnesses.

But Francesca had known she would lose on those points. They were setting up her long-term strategy.

She had been building a connection between them and Bronson. He even "tripped up" during his cross-examination, making himself appear lost and unsure and giving the jury the impression that the prosecutor was a bit of a bully and possibly coercing him into incriminating himself. She didn't care what they thought of her as long as they liked Bronson.

After speaking with him for a few hours before our session was called, I was confident he knew what to do.

Rafa had sat quietly and listened the whole time. When we stood to leave, he shook my hand. "I'm impressed. Are you sure you don't want to come work for me?"

I raised an eyebrow and met his stare. "You can't afford me, Rafa."

He laughed and turned to walk out of the room. "I don't know about that," he tossed back.

"I'm not going to pretend that my brotherhood never skirts the line, Rafa." He stopped and looked back at me. "And I might create a false narrative for the jury to believe, but only through assumption. I will not lie in court."

Rafa cocked his head and studied me for a moment. "Do you think Francesca would?"

He had me there. "No."

"I would never ask her to," he returned. "But everyone has a price, Ash."

"Not if it means betraying a bond that is unbreakable to me."

He watched me again for a moment, then nodded. "*Lealtà prima del sangue*," he said in a low voice. "Loyalty before blood. It's something I understand and respect."

With that, we left the small space and entered the imposing courtroom. A cold room made of marble and wood, with a dour-faced judge, a prosecutor who looked like he thought I was the scum of the earth, and twelve people who I saw as blank slates. No matter what had happened previously in the trial, they were my masterpiece to mold.

With the exception of my home and the clubhouse, this was the place I felt most at home.

The thought startled me because I suddenly realized it was no longer true.

Nora. She was my home. Wherever she was, as long as I was with her, it was home.

Refocusing on my surroundings, I mentally smiled. That wouldn't stop me from kicking ass. And just like that, the charismatic, intelligent Texan emerged.

By the time I was done, I'd convinced the jury that my client was basically an innocent bystander with no knowledge that the art was stolen, no direct ties to the merchandise, and no criminal intent. I'd even managed to infer that the police had so many unsolved smuggling cases that they were going after my client unjustly in order to make themselves look good.

All this without telling a single fabrication...or an outright accusation. The jury was convinced they'd come to these conclusions on their own, and I'd simply given them the tools to figure out the mystery through their own intelligence.

After the verdict, declaring my client not guilty, I told my client to keep his ass out of trouble and packed up, eager to get back to my woman. She'd sent me a text earlier, and I hated that I'd had to wait until now to respond. She hadn't come right out and said anything, but I was willing to bet she'd had an argument with her mom. So I sent her the information for my house and the code I'd already programmed for her.

Rafa stopped me on the courthouse steps with a hand on my shoulder.

I glanced back at him, and he smiled. "You're one hell of a lawyer, Ash. Thank you. And though I know I will never get the call, I still have to put the offer out one more time. If you're ever interested in coming to work for The Family, you will be received with open arms." His grin widened, and he glanced at my extremely expensive, perfectly tailored suit before adding, "And bank accounts."

The corners of my mouth lifted slightly, and I shook my head. "You want me to drain those bank accounts? I'm not opposed to that. But you'll have to get King's permission."

Rafa's expression turned frustrated.

This time, I actually laughed. "Yeah, good luck with that."

9

NORA

My day had started out so well, but it took a decided turn for the worse four hours after I returned home when my mom got back from her luncheon. I hadn't seen her before she left, but since her spot in the garage was right next to mine, she knew I was home and headed straight for my room.

She didn't bother knocking before she flung my door open and stomped over to my bed, where I was lying on my stomach while reading. Tilting my head back, I smiled up at her. "How was your lunch?"

"How was lunch?" she shrieked, planting her hands on her hips. "Is that all you have to say to me after disappearing for an entire night with that...that...thug?"

I set my book to the side with a sigh, then shifted

positions so that I was sitting cross-legged—and she didn't have quite as much of a height advantage. "I told you who was picking me up, Mom. That thug, as you called him, was Eli."

"Elias Prescott III is in a gang?" she asked, her eyes wide.

"The Hounds of Hellfire aren't a gang, Mother. They're a motorcycle club," I corrected, my voice thick with irritation. "One with members like Eli, who's a lawyer. And two doctors who I haven't met yet. I don't think that thug accurately describes men who've earned medical degrees and juris doctorates. Do you?"

"Well, I never," she huffed, twisting her hands together. "A senator's son in a motorcycle club? That's ridiculous."

"Eli is more than his father's son." And I was more than my mother's daughter, but I didn't voice that thought because the only thing that would accomplish was making her even more angry.

"Now you're being ridiculous," she chided. "That boy grew up with all the advantages anyone could ask for, and he walked away from it for a motorcycle club of all things?"

Eli had left his family behind way before he prospected for the Hounds, but that was his story to tell. Not mine. And my parents had to earn the right to hear it—something I worried would never happen with their deeply ingrained biases against everyone they saw as beneath them.

"That boy is a thirty-three-year-old man," I pointed out.

"Well, hopefully he comes to his senses now that he's dating a nice girl like you." She smoothed the material of her skirt. "A summer wedding next year with a senator in attendance would do wonders for your father's next mayoral campaign."

I narrowed my eyes and shook my head. "It's way too soon to be talking about getting married."

"Not if you're spending the entire night out with him," she chided, wagging her finger. "Remember... men won't want to buy the cow if you're giving them the milk for free."

Was it any wonder that I'd still been a virgin when I got advice like that from her since I was twelve?

As soon as she trotted back out of my room, I grabbed my cell and typed out a text. I had no idea if Eli would see it anytime soon, but I was desperate.

> **ME**
>
> I really wish I'd waited for you at the clubhouse. No matter how long you're gone.

It was a while before he responded, but at least I'd been able to avoid my mother and finish my book during that time.

> **ELI**
>
> Head to my house, and I'll meet you there soon.

His offer was a big deal, especially coming from the man who'd told me that he'd never brought a woman there before.

> **ME**
>
> I don't remember how to get there and wouldn't be able to get in.

He sent me a pin with the address, followed by another text.

> **ELI**
>
> Door has an electronic lock. Added a code for you. 0720 followed by the # symbol.

That was a number I could easily remember

since it was my birthday. I didn't know how he knew when it was, same as I never found out how he got my phone number. But I was impressed by the thought he'd put into choosing a code that meant something to me.

ME

Thank you.

Those two words weren't enough to express my gratitude, so I'd just have to come up with a better way when I saw him. Preferably one that involved me stripping that sexy suit from his even sexier body.

After tossing a few things into a weekender bag, I grabbed my purse, keys, and phone. Then I headed out the door, calling, "I'm going to see the man you're hoping will propose soon, Mom."

"If you spend the night again, be sure to set an alarm so you can put on your face before he wakes up."

Since I couldn't remember the last time I'd seen her without makeup, I wasn't surprised by the suggestion. But I was stunned that she didn't lecture me about being home at a decent hour—probably because she was holding out hope that Eli would reconcile with his parents and give her something to brag about at the country club.

Whatever the reason, I took the win. And right on its heels came another since Eli pulled into his driveway right behind me in a Mercedes my father would appreciate. He shot me a sexy smile when he climbed out of the driver's side and flung his suit coat over his shoulder. "Hey, baby girl. Thought for sure you'd beat me here. Seems I forgot to account for how long it'd take you to drive over."

"Considering the little show you're putting on for me." I gestured down the length of his tall body. "I think my timing was perfect."

He prowled toward me, his hazel eyes filled with heat. "Only thing that woulda been better was if you were waiting for me in my bed. Naked."

"That can be arranged."

The last word ended on a yelp when he crouched low enough to press his shoulder against my belly and lift me high into the air. Then he marched to the front door, punched in a code, tossed his suit coat onto a rack against the wall, and headed deeper into the house.

I hadn't come inside when Mark and I followed Eli here in the rig to pick up his truck for our first date, so I was curious about the place he called home. But I didn't get the chance to see much before he dumped me onto the mattress in what I assumed was the primary bedroom.

Pressing my elbows into the plush surface beneath me, I levered up just enough to cast him a playful look. "You're not going to give me the full tour?"

"After," he growled, kicking off his shoes before undoing the buckle on his belt.

I practically panted in anticipation as I got my own personal strip show. When he dropped his dress shirt to the floor, my fingers itched to trace over the black lines of the tattoo etched onto his left side. Also those thick veins in his forearms. And his six-pack abs. Basically, every inch of his amazing body…along with my tongue.

"I think I found a new fetish—suit porn." His brows drew together as he stalked toward me, and I hurried to add, "But only if you're the one who's putting it on or taking it off."

"Damn fucking straight, I'm the only man you're ever gonna see naked." Not wanting to ruin the moment, I decided it was probably best if I didn't point out that sometimes I got stuck on calls when the patient wasn't wearing clothes. I was rewarded for my restraint when Eli undid the button on his pants and dragged the zipper down. "And no other man is ever gonna sink into your sweet pussy, like I'm about to do right now."

I signaled my enthusiasm for that plan by kicking off my shoes and yanking my top over my head. By the time he crawled onto the mattress in only his boxer briefs, I was down to my bra and panties.

"Been thinking about this all damn day," he rasped right before his lips slammed down onto mine.

His kiss started out explosive and built more from there. He devoured my mouth as though he was a starving man and I was the only thing that could satisfy him.

I clung to his shoulders, my knees going up so that his hips were cradled between my legs. His hard length pressed against my core, creating a friction that drove me wild.

"I have, too. Need you," I panted against his lips.

"You're gonna get me, baby girl," he promised. "But first, you earned yourself another spanking."

My inner walls clenched at the thought of him leaving his handprint on my butt cheek again. But I still asked, "How did I do that?"

His hazel eyes burned with possession as he growled, "Two words...suit porn."

"I was only talking about you, which I already

said." Rolling my eyes, I laughed. "You left me all hot and bothered this morning after I watched you get dressed. Then you did it again just climbing out of your car. Whoever you get your suits from definitely deserves a raise."

"Any hint of you with another man makes me see red," he admitted, yanking my hips off the mattress with one hand so he could swat at my butt with the other.

The spanking wasn't as hard as the ones he'd given me last night, but I wasn't expecting it, so I yelped in surprise. "Hey!"

"You want to waste time complaining?" He trailed his lips along my jaw to whisper in my ear. "Or do you want to get straight to me giving you so much pleasure that your screams echo off these walls?"

I let out a little moan when he nipped at my earlobe. "Bring on the orgasms."

He must've loved my response because he captured my mouth in another deep, ravishing kiss. His hands went behind my back to undo the clasp of my bra, then he slid them to the front to cup my bare breasts. He stroked the pads of his thumbs over my nipples, and it felt as though there was a direct line between them and my womb.

Moaning, I arched my back to press my chest deeper into his touch. "If you like that, baby girl, you're gonna fucking love this."

His lips wrapped around one of the pebbled tips, and I shuddered in need. "Eli, yes!"

Every tug of his mouth and teeth sent a streak of pleasure straight to my clit, making me desperate to feel him moving inside me. When he switched to the opposite side to toy with that rounded globe, I wiggled beneath him in an attempt to ease the ache between my legs.

"Is my sweet baby girl's pussy ready to take my big, fat cock?" He punctuated his question by slipping his hand lower and trailing his fingers between my drenched folds. "Based on how wet you are for me, I'd say yes. But I want to hear the words from your perfect lips."

"Yes," I gasped.

"You gotta give me more than that, baby girl."

I stroked my hand up his spine as I murmured, "I need you inside me. Please."

"Good girl."

He made quick work of stripping my panties off my body before shoving his boxer briefs down his legs. But before he settled back between my thighs, he yanked me down the mattress until my pussy was right in front of his mouth. Then his tongue circled my clit while he sank a finger in my tight hole.

I rocked my hips against his face, already desperate to come. As though he knew exactly what I needed, Eli twisted his wrist to hit the perfect spot inside me at the same time as his teeth tugged on my sensitive bundle of nerves.

My climax crashed over me, and I screamed, "Yes, oh yes! Eli!"

He ate me through my release, only tearing his mouth from me to replace it with the tip of his dick after my tremors stopped. I still hadn't fully caught my breath when he plunged deep inside, and I dug my nails into his shoulders while I held on for the wild ride he gave me.

After giving me a moment to adjust to his invasion, he slipped his hands beneath my knees. Then he used his grip to drape my legs over his shoulders until only my shoulder blades and head were left on the mattress. "Time to do a little test of the limberness you bragged about."

This position allowed him to drive deep enough for the tip of his dick to hit my cervix on each powerful thrust. He had all the control, and I could only take what he gave me while I was practically folded in half. Over and over again until I was writhing in ecstasy. "Eli! Yes! Oh yes!"

"I fucking love how your pussy fights to keep my cock inside. Fuck, yes! That's it, baby girl. Come for me."

Between his sensual demand and how his dick hammered into my pussy, I flew apart, screaming his name as I came.

Eli's head reared back, the tendons in his neck standing out as he roared, "Fuck! Oh fuck, baby! Yes!"

The splash of his hot come against my inner walls set me off again. With his face buried in the crook of my neck, Eli kept moving until my tremors subsided. Then he rolled over onto his back without breaking our connection.

"Remind me to sign you up for some yoga classes or something. Gotta keep you flexible if you can bend like that while taking my dick hard."

I never knew a woman could laugh while having a guy's dick inside them, but I wasn't surprised when I giggled. Being with Eli made me so darn happy, I was overflowing with joy.

10

ASH

"Good morning, baby girl," I murmured as I pulled Nora deeper into my body and put my face in her neck to get my fill of her coffee and cinnamon scent.

Then I slid my hand up into her silky, fiery red strands and pulled her hair back to take her mouth in a deep kiss.

"Best way to wake up ever," she said with a sigh.

I turned her onto her back and covered her body with mine before growling, "If you think this is the best, then I'm not doing my job right, baby girl."

After another hour, I was confident I'd proved my point when I had to carry her exhausted, limp body into the shower.

"Good gravy," she muttered when I carried her

out of the shower and admired the red handprints on her tight ass while I dried her off. "I have to work today, and you've just sapped me of all my energy."

Laughing, I placed a kiss on her back, then turned her around and kissed her stomach—silently hoping it would be growing big and round soon. When my mouth roamed lower, she grabbed my head and yanked. "Stay away from my flower, you big brute. It needs a break."

I roared with laughter, almost falling on my ass before I finally caught my breath and stood. "I don't think you can call it a flower anymore, baby girl. Isn't that what they call a virgin pussy?"

Her cheeks turned pink, and she shrugged.

"How about you call it Eli's favorite snack?"

Nora huffed and rolled her eyes, then grinned. "Maybe when you officially meet my mother."

Damn, she was adorable. I loved her so fucking much and almost told her right then, but I was hoping to say the words for the first time when I had her property patch to give her. It was supposed to be done tomorrow, so I wouldn't have to wait long.

"Come on, baby girl. Let's get you ready for work. Got to meet with Ace in an hour anyway."

"Ace?" she repeated curiously.

She didn't ask for more details, knowing I might not be able to tell her anything.

"You're fucking perfect, know that?"

She beamed at me in the mirror as she brushed her hair.

"Nothin' all that exciting. We're looking at buying some local real estate and possibly a couple of businesses. Money guy and the lawman got to do the due diligence first."

Nora giggled. "I like that. Can I call you 'the lawman'?"

"You can call me *your* lawman, baby girl. But be prepared to be fucked up against the nearest wall."

"Hmm, I'll keep that in mind."

I grinned, then swatted her ass, making her hiss from the sting on her tender flesh. It made me hard as fuck, so I hurried out to our bedroom, knowing we both needed to get ready for the day.

I walked into the large closet I'd thought was overkill when I bought the house but now was glad I had it when I saw Nora's reaction. After yanking on a pair of jeans and a T-shirt, I shrugged on my cut and swaggered back into the bedroom.

Nora was staring at the bed, frowning.

"What's up, baby girl?"

"Well...um, I brought my uniform last night because I knew I had to work today."

"Good thinking. So what's got your pretty face lookin' like you swallowed a lemon, darlin'?"

As expected, a smile broke out on her face when I tossed out my Texas accent.

"You have to talk to my mom like that, Eli," she told me in a fit of giggles. "It will kill her that the smooth-talking, rich son of a Texas senator isn't everything she wants you to be."

I chuckled, then circled her waist with my arm and drew her back against my chest so I could place little kisses on her neck and shoulder while inhaling her delicious scent.

"Back up, baby girl. What were you thinkin' about when I came out of the closet?"

"Just that I should have thought to bring more clothes. I'm not ready to go home and face my mom."

I turned her around slowly and cupped her face in my palms. "First, you don't have to go home until you're ready. Is that clear? Second, you need anything, I'll buy it for you," I told her, giving her a look that shut her up when she opened her mouth to argue. "Get used to me spoiling you, baby girl. I intend to give you everything."

Her face had gone soft, and she went up on her

tiptoes to give me a sweet kiss. "I don't need anything but you, Eli."

I brushed my mouth over hers before releasing her and walking over to my dresser to grab my keys and wallet. "Get dressed, baby girl. Gonna make you some breakfast."

The French toast was almost done when she padded into the kitchen. I stretched out my arm, and she walked straight to me so I could hold her close while I flipped the bread.

"Your kitchen is amazing," she said with a blissful sigh. I glanced down to see her looking around with a dreamy expression.

"Glad you like it, baby girl. But feel free to change anything you want." I had to let her go to scoop the toast out of the pan and put it on plates, so I didn't notice her stunned expression until I'd set them on the table and turned around.

"What?"

Nora blinked a few times, then brushed her hair over her shoulder and licked her lips.

"Baby girl," I growled. "You will never make it to work if you keep licking your lips like that. You know it turns me the fuck on."

She swallowed hard and squeezed her thighs

together, making me groan. I forced myself to turn away and grab the butter and syrup.

"You want me to make changes?" she asked softly when I stepped out of the walk-in pantry.

"Of course," I replied without thinking as I set the syrup on the table.

"To your house?"

Her tone was oddly insistent, so I turned around and looked at her, crossing my arms over my chest. "It's your house, too, baby girl. So do whatever you want with it."

She stared at me with her mouth open and her blue eyes round as saucers. "D-d-did...did you just ask me to move in with you?" she sputtered.

I laughed, and she glared at me. "No, baby girl. I'm not asking."

"Oh." Her shoulders drooped, and she looked sad and confused at the same time.

"C'mere, Nora," I ordered, holding out my hand.

She cautiously walked toward me, and when she was close enough, I reached out and grabbed her shirt, yanking her up against me. "Wasn't asking because it's a done deal, baby girl. You *are* moving in with me."

Her skin flushed, and she smiled brightly. "I

should probably put up a fight and tell you that you can't order me around."

"But...?"

"But I don't want to," she yelled before throwing her arms around me and peppering my face with kisses.

It was another hour before we got out the door.

Feeling smug and happy, I strolled into the clubhouse less than ten minutes later. Ace looked up when I entered his office and frowned. "Well, don't you look like a man who spent the night fucking his woman?"

"Jealous?" I snarked.

Ace looked at his desk and picked up a sheaf of papers, and I almost didn't hear him when he muttered, "Yes."

Curiously, I inquired, "Of the fucking or the girl?"

He sighed. "Both, I guess."

"I get it, man."

"Yeah. Okay, enough of this bullshit, we've got work to do."

We went through potential properties for a couple of hours, then headed to King's office to give him our recommendations.

Before we reached his door, my cell vibrated. I

checked the caller ID and frowned when I saw a number that looked familiar, but I didn't recognize. I let it go to voicemail, but then I got a text alert before the number called back again.

> **UNKNOWN**
> It's Mark. ANSWER!

I immediately hit the accept button, my heart racing because this could only be about Nora.

"Mark?"

"Fucking hell, Ash! They came out of nowhere! I-I-tried to stop them!"

"Mark!" I shouted. "Calm the fuck down and tell me what's going on!"

"They took Nora!"

11

NORA

One minute, Mark had been teasing me about finally having my first boyfriend, and the next, a truck sideswiped his side of the ambulance. He'd thrown the rig into park and jumped out so fast, I hadn't understood what was happening until it was too late.

A van skidded to a stop only a few feet next to me, and it took me a moment to realize the driver was wearing a ski mask. In June. When it was eighty-three degrees outside and humid. I turned to call Mark's name, but he was yelling at the guy who hit us and didn't hear me.

By the time I undid my seat belt, three other guys had piled out of the van. They were all wearing ski masks, too.

"Holy guacamole, this cannot be good," I muttered.

I was quickly proven right when one of them yanked my door open and pointed a gun at my head. "Get out."

"Okay." I slowly climbed out of the rig, careful not to make any sudden movements. Taking care of Ink's bullet wound the other day didn't mean that I wanted to end up with one of my own. Ever.

"You're coming with us," he growled as soon as my feet hit the ground.

"I'm what?" I squeaked.

He wrapped his hand around my wrist and started to tug me toward the van. Even as I struggled against his hold, he turned to one of the other guys and ordered, "Grab whatever shit you think she'll need from the back of the ambulance."

Realization hit me...I was being taken by these men so I could provide medical care to someone. To an unknown location where my patient could be fighting for their life from something I couldn't treat. And if they died, odds were good that these men wouldn't be happy.

I started fighting as though my life counted on getting away from them—because it likely did. "Mark, help!"

My partner rounded the front of the ambulance just as the guy holding my arm lifted me off my feet to toss me into the van.

"No, stop! You can't take her," Mark yelled.

The driver turned in his seat and aimed a gun at me. "Come any closer, and I'll shoot her."

Mark stopped, holding his hands high in the air, his eyes agonized as he stared at me. "Take me instead."

"No way in hell," the guy who'd manhandled me growled. "She'll be a fuck of a lot easier to handle than you."

The man who'd been ordered to grab supplies dumped a bunch of stuff into the back of the van before climbing in with me. I was relieved to see my trauma bag was one of the items since it had most of what I needed on a variety of calls, and I had a feeling that I could use whatever help I could get.

On that thought, I shouted, "Call Eli! Tell him what happened."

"Will do. Stay safe," Mark answered, a muscle jumping in his jaw as the two remaining men climbed into the van. Then they slammed the door shut, and the driver stepped on the gas.

From my safety training, I knew that being taken to a secondary location was bad. Getting shot in the head would've been worse, though. As long as I was still alive, I had hope. And a secret weapon who would look for me and had an entire club to help.

"Who's Eli?" the guy who'd manhandled me into the van asked.

"My boyfriend." I'd been awkward when Mark had used the term earlier to describe him since we hadn't really made our relationship official. And calling Eli any word that started with boy seemed like an odd choice, but under these circumstances, it was a heck of a lot better than explaining he was the biker I was sleeping with…and was supposed to move in with if I made it out of this situation alive.

If these guys knew about my connection to the Hounds of Hellfire, either it'd scare them into letting me go or make them freak out enough that they'd decide to get rid of me right away to limit their chances of getting caught.

"Do what we say, and you just might get the chance to see your boyfriend again."

I rubbed my damp palms against my thighs and asked, "Are you taking me to someone who needs medical care?"

"Keep your mouth shut until we get where we're going."

I pressed my lips into a flat line and twisted my hands together while I did what he ordered. The ride felt as though it took forever, but it was probably only ten minutes later when we pulled in front of an abandoned warehouse in the industrial sector of the town between mine and Eli's.

I didn't put up a fight when I was dragged from the van. Or when I was shoved through the rusted door that the driver opened for the guy who was manhandling me yet again.

The place was filthy, and the lighting was awful, but there was no missing the man sprawled on the floor. The piece of clothing pressed against his abdomen was covered in blood, and a small red pool had gathered beneath him. Even from here, I could see how pale his skin was.

As I approached, I took in the perspiration dotting his forehead and upper lip. "What happened to him?"

The guy behind me shoved me forward before answering, "He got shot."

"In the stomach?"

"Yeah."

I rushed over to the injured man and dropped to my knees next to him, gently moving the blood-soaked shirt up so I could see where the bullet wound was. "Did it happen here?"

"Why do you want to know?" one of the guys carrying in the supplies snarled.

"Because I need to know if you moved him or if he was mobile on his own," I explained. "With where he was hit, there's a high risk of spinal damage."

"Didn't happen here," the man I'd coined their ringleader in my head answered. "He was able to climb into the van, but we had to help him out when we got here."

"How long ago did this all happen?"

"Thirty minutes ago." He raked his fingers through his hair. "We were lucky to come across your ambulance so quickly."

All of the worries that I'd had when Eli asked me to treat Ink's bullet wound were multiplied. This situation was worse in so many ways. I didn't have access to all of the medical equipment available to me in the Hounds of Hellfire clinic. This guy had been shot in his abdomen, not his thigh. And instead of having Eli and Echo there to help me, I had four men with guns who were ready to shoot me if anything went wrong. Even if it wasn't my fault.

"Your friend really does need a hospital," I

insisted. "He got shot in one of the worst possible places. If his liver, spleen, or intestines were hit, the internal bleeding is life-threatening. And even if I can stop it, there's a much higher risk of infection due to the bacteria in his digestive tract."

"You tell us what you need to fix him, and I'll send a couple of the guys out to get it for you."

I tilted my head back to glare at him. "What I need is a doctor. And not just any kind—a surgeon. I'm only an EMT, not even a paramedic. You would've been better off if you had taken Mark. He was a combat medic. If you're not willing to take your friend to the nearest emergency room, he would've been your best bet at saving his life."

"You better hope you're wrong." He used the barrel of his gun to point at his wounded friend and then me again as he threatened, "Because your fates are tied together now. If he dies, you die."

I'd just found Eli and fell head over heels in love with him. I needed to make it out of this alive so I could tell him those three little words that I'd never said to another man other than my father.

"Then take the gun away from my head so I can focus on what I need to do." I pointed at my trauma bag. "And bring that over here while one of your men checks the stuff they took from my rig to see if there are any pain meds. Your friend is gonna need them."

As I began my examination, I sent up a little prayer that Eli would find me before things got worse for me.

12

ASH

I roared in outrage, bringing Blaze and King running out of their offices.

"What the fuck?" Blaze asked, but Ace just shook his head and shrugged while I demanded that Mark give me every detail.

"Shit," King grunted. "Sounds like Nora's been snatched."

I nodded, and he dashed back into his office.

"Did they take her phone?" I barked at Mark.

"It's in the fucking ambulance. Shit! Shit! How did I let this happen?"

"Don't have time to reassure you, Mark. But for fuck's sake, what were you gonna do without getting yourself fucking killed? Send me your location and any description of the guys, the vehicle, which direction, whatever you can remember."

I hung up just as King returned, and Kevlar, Cross, and Fallon came jogging toward us from the other direction.

"Nora's been taken?" Kevlar asked.

"Ran her fucking ambulance off the road and took her," I informed them as I forwarded Mark's text to Wizard. "They grabbed her medical bag, so I'm guessing they want her to treat someone."

Fallon's expression faltered. "What if she doesn't have the training for the person's wounds?"

I scowled at him. "What the fuck do you think, asshole?"

"What can we do?" Cross asked.

"Get suited up," King instructed. "Soon as Wizard has something, head out."

Blaze was texting and looked up. "Need more backup?"

"Should be good, but keep a couple on standby," I replied over my shoulder as we all followed Kevlar to the armory.

Just as I finished arming myself with a couple of guns, a knife, and a few other lethal items, my phone rang.

"Tell me," I demanded when I answered Wizard's call.

"Got the van on traffic cams. You got any kind of tracking on Nora? Anything at all?"

I was about to tell him no when a light bulb went off. "Holy shit. I forgot. She's got a fob to my house." I'd given it to her in case the keypad ever went on the fritz.

"Give me a sec...okay, sending you a location."

"Owe you, man."

"Nah. You'd do the same for my woman."

True.

"Let's ride," I grunted as I jogged from the armory to the garage and out to my bike, which was parked in a lot on the side of the clubhouse.

It took fifteen minutes to get close to the area the GPS indicated as Nora's location. We parked half a mile away and hoofed the rest on foot to stay stealth.

At the indicated coordinates was an old warehouse. The windows were just below shoulder height with no bars or deterrents of any kind. Wizard's satellite scan hadn't hinted at any kind of security system either.

The motherfuckers were clearly morons for picking a place that provided no protection, making it easy for us to get inside undetected.

I motioned for Kevlar and Cross to go around the side of the building, while Fallon and I breached from the back. We were prepared to climb the windows but found the front door unlocked.

"Unbelievable," Fallon grunted.

"Stupid as shit, but I'm not complaining."

The door opened to a small room that appeared empty, so we entered but stayed in the shadows.

I froze when I heard Nora's scared but determined voice. "If you're not willing to take your friend to the nearest emergency room, he would've been your best bet at saving his life."

"You better hope you're wrong," a man barked. "Because your fates are tied together now. If he dies, you die."

Fury ripped through me, and I took a step forward, only to be yanked back by Fallon. "Calm the fuck down, or you're gonna get her killed."

I sucked in several deep breaths and nodded once I was in control. We silently moved toward a cracked door, and when I nudged it open a little, I saw four big guys huddled around my girl. She was on the ground, looking over an injured man while one of them held a gun to her head.

That fucker's life had just ended.

When a second man moved to get her bag, I knocked on the doorframe.

"Howdy," I drawled as I walked a few steps into the room.

All of the men swiveled their heads in my direction, and the one beside Nora dropped to the ground with a bullet between his eyes, another crumpled over Nora's bag with a hole in the side of his head. The last two managed to get their guns in their hands before they also dropped like lead weights, hitting the ground from lethal gunshots.

Nora screamed, but not at the sight of four men being shot right in front of her. She jumped to her feet and came running at me full speed.

"Fuck, baby girl," I grunted when my arms closed around her. "Scared the motherfucking shit outta me."

"I knew you'd find me," she said between sobs as she squeezed the life out of my torso.

"Always, baby girl," I reassured her—and myself. "Always."

"I-I"—she hiccupped—"I don't want to have any regrets, though."

"Regrets?" I echoed as I used a finger under her chin to tilt her face up.

"I love you," she blurted. "I should have said it before."

The words stunned me, and when I didn't speak right away, doubt began to creep into her bright blue pools.

I shoved one of my hands into her fiery tresses and held her head back so she couldn't look away. "I love the fuck outta you, baby girl," I growled, my expression dead serious. "More than life. So, if you ever scare the shit out of me like this again, you won't be able to sit for a fucking week. Got it?"

Nora giggled, and I couldn't help smiling in return.

A groan of anguish caught our attention, and I glanced over to see Kevlar and Cross kneeling over the injured man.

"Worth trying to get him to the hospital?" I asked.

"Yes," Nora snapped. "I get why the other two are dead, but it's my job to save lives, Eli."

"Fuck, baby girl. You're gonna make it damn hard for me to do my job sometimes."

She shrugged. "But you love me, so you'll get over it."

I laughed before glancing over at Kevlar and

Cross. "Take the van, and I'll get someone to come grab your hogs."

Then I ordered Fallon to stay with the motorcycles while I took my woman home.

The ride back to our house helped me calm down, especially since the feel of her wrapped around me on my bike was a constant reminder that she was safe.

After parking in the garage, I dismounted, then didn't bother with helping her down. I just scooped her into my arms and stalked into the house, right to our bedroom.

Setting her on her feet, I walked her backward to the bed. By the time we reached it, I'd stripped her naked.

"Stay right here," I ordered before spinning on my heel and stalking into my closet. The items I wanted were tucked away on a shelf I knew she couldn't reach. After retrieving them, I returned and grunted in approval when I saw that she'd stayed exactly where I put her.

"Very good, baby girl," I crooned.

Her blush spread all the way down to her pussy, and I had to remind myself that I needed to do something before I devoured her.

"Been wanting to see you like this since the moment you walked into that house."

"Naked?" she laughed.

I shook my head and held out one of the things I'd brought from the closet. "In nothing but my brand."

Nora's hand trembled when she reached out to take the leather vest. "You want me to be your old lady?"

"Who the fuck else would I want?" I asked with a smirk. "Didn't you hear the part where I said that I love you?"

She beamed a smile and handed me the vest to hold while she slipped her arms into it.

I looked her over, then grabbed the sides and hauled her body against mine. "Fuck, yeah," I growled. "Looks even better than I thought it would." I kissed her deeply, then chuckled when she whined in protest. "Patience, baby girl. There's somethin' else I want you to be."

She grinned and shrugged. "Whatever it is, I'll say yes."

"Good," I grunted. "'Cause I wasn't asking." I picked up her left hand and slid a diamond ring that, while beautiful, didn't come close to sparkling as bright as my girl. "Gonna be my wife, too," I stated before taking her lips in another soul-stealing kiss that had us both shaking with need when it ended.

"Like I said," she panted. "Even if you didn't ask. My answer is yes."

"Love you so fucking much, baby girl."

"Good thing I love you too because it makes us a perfect match."

EPILOGUE
NORA

Planning a wedding with my mother was a nightmare that I never should have signed up for. From the guest list to my dress—and everything in between—we hadn't agreed on a single thing.

This was supposed to be the happiest time of my life, but each time I came home to Eli after working on plans with her, I was sad, angry, or frustrated. And today was no different.

The menu Eli and I wanted was simple compared to my mother's tastes. She wanted a plated dinner with roasted rack of lamb, seared scallops, and mushroom ragout as options for our guests. She had been horrified to learn that we'd picked an Italian buffet instead, a decision my groom refused to budge on since he wanted me to have my favorite food on our special day.

If only my mother was as concerned about my preferences and not what her friends would think about our wedding. The few we'd allowed her to invite since, according to her, the one hundred guests on our side wasn't nearly enough. Which was a number I insisted on because I wasn't going to take seats from Eli's side to make her happy. It was more important to me that we were surrounded by his found family when we celebrated our marriage.

"It's a good thing you're a lawyer," I announced as I walked through the door of our house. "I'm going to need one when I finally give in to the temptation to kill my mother."

Wrapping his arms around me, my soon-to-be husband pulled me in for a hug that I very much needed. "What's wrong, baby girl?"

I pressed my cheek against his broad chest and mumbled, "Just my mom being her usual self."

He slid his hand between our bodies to cup my still flat belly. "Did she say something bad about our happy news?"

"No, I didn't tell her." Thinking about the argument we got into, I sniffled. "She was already upset because I wouldn't cave over the location for the reception, even though the country club had a cancellation for our wedding date. The bride was the daughter of one of her close friends, and she just found out her groom had been cheating on her with her maid of honor. She barely said sorry to her friend before hanging up to call the club to see if we could slide into the newly opened spot."

"Sounds like her," he muttered.

"I didn't want to risk that being why she reacted badly to the news that her daughter is going to walk down the aisle while pregnant." I shook my head with a watery laugh. "But maybe I should have. At least her social circle will be too busy gossiping about that poor girl to say much about us."

Eli hadn't been happy when I insisted on telling my mom without him there. But she still hadn't gotten over the fact that we weren't inviting his parents to the wedding—which she blamed him for—so I thought it would be easier to tell her on my own.

"I don't like you being so stressed. Especially while you're carrying my baby."

I tilted my head back to smile up at him as I teased, "Let's be honest...you wouldn't be much happier with my mom's shenanigans, even if I wasn't pregnant."

"Damn straight," he confirmed without an ounce

of shame. "My job as your man is to make your life easier, which is why I booked us a flight to Vegas tonight. I've had enough of this bullshit. We're going to get married, just the two of us and our little bean that you're carrying in your belly."

My mom would have a conniption fit if we eloped, but that didn't stop me from crying, "Yes!"

He brushed his lips over mine. "Glad you're on board with the plan because I've already packed our shit, and we need to head to the airport."

"Let's go, then."

Before I could tug him toward the door, he jerked his chin in the direction of our bedroom. "Got to grab our bags first, baby girl."

"Did you pack my wedding dress?"

"I sure as fuck did," he confirmed.

It was a good thing that I kept it in a black garment bag so he didn't accidentally see it. I wanted to surprise him in my gown on our wedding day, which was apparently happening much sooner than we originally planned. "Do we have a reservation at a wedding chapel?"

He flashed me a smug grin. "Yup, and it's the one you got all dreamy-eyed over when you saw that photo spread in your bridal magazine."

"Really?" I squealed, clapping while I bounced

on my toes. "The one with the three sisters who run it? And the florist is married to Griffith Thorne, the lead singer of Rising Phoenix?"

"Not sure about all that, but I got the name from the article. It was easy to find since you read it so many times that the page is practically worn out."

"Oh my gosh, this is going to be so amazing. Getting married there will be worth all of the crap my mom is going to dish out when we get back."

Eli quirked a brow. "Thought me becoming your husband would be enough for that. Not to mention the wedding night we're about to have."

"Definitely," I agreed with a grin.

Having Griffith Thorne sing as I walked down the aisle—a surprise Eli somehow managed to arrange—didn't top the moment the Elvis impersonator announced us as man and wife. Or the ridiculous number of orgasms I had during the twenty-four hours following our ceremony.

Too bad we had to cut the trip short when Ink called with an urgent request—the woman he wanted to claim needed a lawyer.

EPILOGUE

ASH

"Wow, Jelly Bean. You look gorgeous," I complimented my daughter when she walked into the living room. *Damn, how did she get to be sixteen?*

"*Must* you call her that?" Deidre whined. Nora's mother had mellowed over the years, but she still made me want to toss her out on her ass sometimes.

Jennalynn and I rolled our eyes at each other, then grinned.

"Thanks, Daddy. But…do I have to wear it?" She glanced down at the puffy pink princess dress and screwed her face up in disgust. It was completely wrong for my "rocker-chick"—her words—daughter's style.

"Of course not, Jelly Bean."

Diedre gasped. "You agreed to let her have a debutante ball when she turned sixteen!"

"Yes, Mom," Nora sighed as she sashayed into the room. "Jen agreed to the party." I winked at her and held out my hand, beckoning her to come to me. She smiled and sauntered over, letting me pull her down into my lap. "But we didn't commit to a particular kind of dress, or the guest list you gave me, or the decorations you picked out."

"Did you learn anything from our wedding, Diedre?" I drawled. "You push..."

Nora grinned. "We push back."

"Or run away," Jennalynn snickered, then huffed, "Don't get me wrong, that's sounding really freaking great right about now."

I turned my wife's face toward me and pressed my lips to hers, only pulling away when Jennalynn muttered, "I'm right here, guys. Cool it on the making out."

"Yes," Diedre snipped. "*Must* you do that?"

"Yes," I told her matter-of-factly. "Woulda thought you'd get over it, considering it's how you got four kick-ass grandbabies."

Diedre sniffed, but her face softened when she

looked at Jennalynn. "You do look beautiful, my dear."

"I look like a cupcake, Grandma," Jennalynn snorted.

"You look perfect. Don't you want to catch the eye of your handsome prince?" Nora's mom asked with a slightly dreamy tone.

Nora, Jennalynn, and I all burst into laughter.

"Nah, Grandma. I'm lookin' for the guy up the road who has tattoos and rides a motorcycle." She winked at me adorably, so I didn't comment that she would never be dating.

Nora tilted her head, studying our daughter with a secretive smile. "Why don't you show your grandmother the dress you picked out?"

Jennalynn's face lit up, and she bounced out of the room.

"Honestly," Diedre huffed. "What *are* you teaching that girl, Nora?"

"To be herself. No matter what anyone else thinks."

I fucking adored my wife.

"Daddy!" Vivienne screamed. A second later, our four-year-old came barreling into the room with a terrified expression and chocolate all over her face.

"Vivi! You are in so much fucking trouble!" Garner—our twelve-year-old son—shouted.

I winced as Nora and Diedre gasped like pearl-clutching old ladies. It was me who was gonna be in a shit ton of trouble.

Vivi ran over and threw herself at Nora, burying her face in her stomach.

When Garner burst into the room, he glared daggers at the little thief and stalked across the room. He stopped in front of us and shoved his hand onto his hips. "That was the last of my Halloween candy!"

Vivi turned her head—leaving a smear of chocolate on Nora's T-shirt—and blinked her big blue eyes at him as giant tears rolled down her cheeks.

She was a master at puppy dog eyes and heartbreaking tears, which was why she had every man in this house wrapped around her little fingers.

"Sorry, G," she said in a trembling voice. "I didn't know it was yours." Then she leaned in and whispered, "I thought it was Shep's."

"Ugh," Diedre moaned. She hated that all our kids went by nicknames.

Personally, I enjoyed her pain, but I kept that to myself.

"It was mine," fourteen-year-old Shepherd muttered from the corner where he'd been practically hiding behind a book since his grandma arrived. "G stole it first. So serves you right, bro."

Before anyone could say anything else, Jennalynn strolled back in.

"What is that?" Diedre screeched.

"Well, Mom," Nora said in an "announcer" voice. "This gorgeous model is wearing a vintage-inspired satin A-line gown. The strapless dress has boning in the corset and lovely, handcrafted details. As you can see, there is ruching at the top of the skirt before it flows to the floor in front, with a slit up the left side and a court train in the back. To add flair to this ensemble, made so incredibly beautiful by the model, are black lace gloves that end on the biceps with intricate detailing."

Jennalynn was beaming and walking around the living room as if she were on a runway.

I might have laughed if I wasn't so fucking speechless. When did my little girl grow the fuck up?

She turned around, and her leg flashed between the thigh-high slit. I jumped to my feet, making sure to keep Nora and Vivi from falling to the ground. "Not a chance in hell, Jelly Bean!" I growled. "You are not wearing that."

"Finally, we agree for once," Diedre sniffed. "But you might have used more appropriate language."

I threw her a withering scowl, and she shut up.

My daughter's face crumpled and tears welled in her eyes, making me feel like the world's biggest jackass. "You don't think it looks good on me, Daddy?"

I sighed and walked over to her, pulling her into my arms. "Of course I do, Jelly Bean. You look amazing."

"Then why—"

"Because I'm not going to let some horny teenage punks drool over my sweet, beautiful girl."

"But Daddy—"

"No. I'm sorry, but—"

"She's growing up, Eli," Nora interrupted. "Soon, she'll be dating. You're going to have to accept it sometime."

I frowned at her. "Like hell. There will be no boys." I turned my glare down to my daughter. "No dating. Not until I'm dead."

Nora sighed. "What if I sew the slit so it starts at her knee?"

Jennalynn's face brightened. "Please, Daddy?"

My resolve loosened.

"Please?"

"Shit," I muttered.

Jennalynn squealed and threw her arms around

me in the kind of hug she used to give me when she was still Vivi's age. "Thank you! Thank you!"

"Really, Nora," Diedre huffed. "Could you at least talk her into a soft pink or maybe a baby blue? They would bring out her eyes and soften the whole...ensemble."

"I already talked her into elegant black, Mom," Nora replied dryly. "Be grateful it's not the blood red or hot pink and black she wanted."

"She looks bweeutiful!" Vivi shouted, clapping her hands.

"Really, Dad?" I looked over at Shep, who was shaking his head sadly.

"I can't believe you caved," G added in a disappointed voice.

"Talk to me when you have daughters, boys."

Shep snorted, "Never gonna happen. Women are too much trouble."

Everyone but G laughed. Instead, he gave his brother a sharp nod in solidarity. They were in for a wake-up call when they met the right woman.

Jennalynn kissed my cheek, then went to pester her grandma into admitting that she secretly liked the dress. Nora sauntered over and wrapped her arms around my torso. Dropping her head back, she smiled up at me. "Thank you, Eli."

I bent my neck and put my lips on her ear before growling, "You know you're going to pay for this tonight, baby girl."

She shivered, and I palmed one of her ass cheeks, giving it a firm squeeze.

"Wook! Daddy's playing gwab azz!" Vivi shrieked before peals of laughter erupted from her cute little mouth.

"Who taught that to my precious grandbaby?" Diedre gasped.

I put my head in Nora's neck to hide my chuckle while her shoulders shook from her silent mirth.

"If I'd known this was how my life would turn out after I met you, I'd have snatched you up and taken off the moment we met," I murmured.

"It's not like you took much longer than that," Nora giggled.

"When a Hound of Hellfire finds the woman for him, we don't fuck around, baby girl. We get a property patch on her back, a ring on her finger, and a baby in her belly."

Nora sighed sweetly. "Well, then. Good thing I fell in love with one."

Want to find out why Ink's woman needs a lawyer? Find out in Ink!

Curious about the wedding chapel where they get married in Vegas? It's from the Vegas, Baby series!

And if you join our newsletter, you'll get a FREE copy of The Virgin's Guardian, which was banned on Amazon.

ABOUT THE AUTHOR

The writing duo of Elle Christensen and Rochelle Paige team up under the Fiona Davenport pen name to bring you sexy, insta-love stories filled with alpha males. If you want a quick & dirty read with a guaranteed happily ever after, then give Fiona Davenport a try!

Printed in Great Britain
by Amazon